THE MAY DAY
MYSTERY

THE MAY DAY
MYSTERY

OCTAVUS ROY COHEN

COACHWHIP PUBLICATIONS
Greenville, Ohio

TO

JAMES SAXON CHILDERS

The May Day Mystery, by Octavus Roy Cohen
© 2025 Coachwhip Publications edition
Cover image: Oakland Chapel, Alcorn State University, MS
    (Library of Congress Prints and Photographs Division)

First published 1929
Octavus Roy Cohen, 1891-1959
CoachwhipBooks.com

ISBN 1-61646-604-9
ISBN-13 978-1-61646-604-6

CHAPTER I

A warm flower-scented breeze caressed the campus of Marland University with a promise of early summer. From the buildings grouped about the athletic bowl came the hum of classroom work, but the magic of a perfect first of May had affected students and professors alike.

May Day is of outstanding importance in the scholastic year of a Southern college. It marks definitely the end of a long grind; it comes quietly and unobtrusively and students who—on April thirtieth—have looked upon the semester as never-ending are suddenly awakened to realization that in a very short time there will be an exodus and the great buildings will become mere hollow shells. Freshmen are elated—seniors saddened—by the imminence of the year's end.

And this May Day was perfect. Spring had proved tardy; April had alternately frowned and wept. The college had trudged to and from classes somewhat drearily and there had been slight interest in the approach of the end of the scholastic year.

But this morning everything changed. A brilliant sun smiled down from an unflecked sky; spring flowers peeped flirtatiously from the hillsides; groups of students lolled under the trees chatting idly—or not talking at all. In some of the classrooms certain seekers after knowledge succumbed to the gentle lure of the day and frankly dozed. Queerly enough they were not rebuked by their instructors. Yesterday this somnolent indifference would have provoked stern and caustic rebuke, but to-day the bars were down. Spring and summer had arrived hand in hand and Marland extended an enthusiastic and uncritical welcome.

The campus was a riot of color; of fresh, delicate green; of gloriously tinted flowers; of gay spring dresses. The young men rambled from building to building in the frank negligee of sport shirts, collars open at the throat and neckties dangling some three or four inches below their appointed places. In the Bowl a dozen or so young men tossed a baseball. On the tennis court a game of mixed doubles was languidly in progress. The grounds keeper was indifferently scraping the cinder track for the class track and field meet which was scheduled for the afternoon . . . but no one seemed excited. It was a day for dreaming; for idly wandering thoughts. To-day was the first of May. It meant something—though no one knew exactly what. Yesterday had meant nothing. To-morrow would mean even less. But this day. . . .

Twelve hundred students of both sexes succumbed to the spell. Worries were dissipated. Spring had come late to this jewel-like campus in mid-Alabama; but had atoned, in the glory of its coming, for all its tardiness. It was a day for emotions rather than thoughts; a glorious, sleepy, sensuous day when one was glad merely to be alive, and when final exams—so perilously close—were matters of small consequence.

Over on the hill a scant quarter mile beyond the Bowl stood the women's dormitory, and immediately before it was a lilac bush in radiant blossom. A girl stepped from the hallway into the sunlight and paused by the lilac bush. Then, with the assured deliberation of a senior, she proceeded to violate a college rule.

Antoinette Peyton picked a spray of lilac.

She did not perform her misdeed surreptitiously. She plucked the flower boldly, indifferent to any eyes which might behold her. Then she gazed across a tiny, verdant valley toward the knoll upon which were situated the academic buildings of the University.

Tony Peyton was a pretty girl. She was more than a pretty girl. There was strength of character in her vivid face with its tiny, scarlet mouth and great, lustrous black eyes. She gave an impression of gorgeous vitality. She touched the sprig of lilac to her mouth—and smiled. She smiled into the sprig, and the campus smiled back at her. It seemed that all the world must love that quick, shy, sensitive smile; that creasing of red lips; the tiny crinkling of the eyes, the ecstatic indrawing of breath.

The ground dropped abruptly away from the dormitory entrance. Below lay a miniature valley, forested with tall and stately pines and carpeted by delicate new flowers. In that little valley were quiet nooks and cozy corners which Tony had learned to know intimately and affectionately during her four years at Marland. There wasn't a tree or a blade of grass which did not have for her a heart-warming association. She had loved the valley as a freshman; it had become part of her during the years which followed, and now even the glory of a perfect May Day could not drive from her heart a feeling of sadness that all too soon she was to say Good-by.

She stared off across the tops of the pine trees toward the knoll on which the academic buildings reared their imposing forms. All of a pattern; red brick and white stone: nine of them standing like indomitable sentinels about the natural stadium which had been converted into the Bowl. Four buildings toward the east and four toward the west, and in the middle the fine, new four-story main building of which Marland was so justly proud. It wasn't

a big college—its total enrollment was less than twelve
hundred—but it was proud. Its campus was mellow with
rich Southern tradition; its archives yielded records of
undergraduates who had gone off in the first bitter days of
'61 to join the Confederate forces; in the hall of Old Main
was its World War Roll of Honor. There were records, too,
of graduates who had risen to positions of importance in
the fields of science and art.

It was a staunch, solid school; inordinately and justifi-
ably proud of itself; jealous of its scholastic standing and
integrity; pleased with the respect accorded it by national
college authorities. And perhaps the students attached just
a wee bit too much importance to the eminence recently
achieved by the Marland football and track teams. Just a
little bit too much importance . . . but this morning Tony
Peyton could understand that, because as she looked down
into the almost empty Bowl she saw in her mind's eye
a picture which had impressed itself indelibly upon her
eighteen months before when Marland's greatest gridiron
team, under the leadership of Larry Welch, had smashed
and battered its way to a legitimate claim to the mythical
national championship. That had been a day: twenty thousand fanatics gone wild in the Bowl; a riot of color and a
welter of sound . . . and that night the rolling topography
of the campus had been dotted with bonfires while the
students celebrated. . . .

Tony glanced at her wrist watch and sighed. With a
conscious effort she rid herself of the spell. With a quick,
eager stride she started down the hill into the valley which
must be crossed before one could mount the other hill—
the hill upon which the college buildings stood.

She walked firmly, the soft breeze brazenly touching
the delicate curves of her slim, boyish figure. All Marland
loved that figure. It had flashed on the basketball floor

through four brilliant seasons; it had been revealed intimately to the spectators of co-ed swimming meets; it had graced delicate evening gowns at fraternity dances. Even Tony's classmates had never overcome the habit of turning to look after her as she passed. There was something irresistible in her exquisite vividity.

She moved through the tiny valley, head thrown back, sprig of lilac held in her right hand, lips moving slightly as she hummed a popular melody. The magic of the day was upon her and she approached the Hill with a feeling of reluctance that the spell must be broken.

And then—quite suddenly—she stopped. For a few seconds she stood motionless, lithe body tense.

Just before her was a huge oak tree. Tony knew that particular tree; it stood sentinel before a forest nook affectionately known by all students at Marland as the Bower; a tiny, secluded spot sheltered by giant trees, carpeted with violets and embowered in honeysuckle.

Voices came to her from that nook: voices of a man and a girl. Tony's teeth pressed tight together and a startled, worried expression leaped into her eyes. She was afraid—but she wasn't sure.

A man in yonder—with a girl. Nothing in that to dispel the glory of the day. It would have been a matter for more wonder had the Bower been unoccupied. But she fancied that she knew the voices . . . the man's voice; the girl's sweetly shrill answers. Then there was silence.

Tony was worried. She wanted to be sure—yet the interior of the Bower was concealed from the eyes of casual passers-by. If one wished to investigate, one was compelled to intrude. Students had assisted nature by training honeysuckle vines so that the Bower was very secluded indeed.

She was of no mind to interrupt a campus romance. Unless . . . She remained motionless for several minutes;

her face a study in worried concentration. Why didn't they speak again? She wished to be sure. She thought. . . .

And then her doubt vanished. From behind the shelter of trees and vines came a man's voice: rich and soft and freighted with caresses.

"Little sweetheart," he said, "you're the most bewitching thing I've ever seen."

Tony's lips pressed to a firm, angry line. It was Pat Thayer all right: Pat making love, in his suave, polished, deferentially superior way—to some one.

But even yet Tony did not move. She was afraid she knew. . . .

Then she heard the childish voice of Thayer's companion: a voice which trembled with the eagerness of a first girlish passion—

"Oh, Pat," said the girl, "you—you're so *wonderful!*"

Tony's face grew stern. It was plain that she was bitterly angry.

She hesitated no longer. She circled the great oak tree and shoved aside the curtain of honeysuckle vines.

The man met her eyes. But he continued to hold the girl tightly in his arms. He smiled sardonically at the intruder over the fluffy golden hair of his companion.

"And who," he inquired with mocking politeness—"Who invited you, Tony?"

CHAPTER II

There was fierce hostility in the glance which passed between Tony Peyton and the tall, too-well-groomed young man. The fluffy little girl whom Pat had been cuddling in his arms disentangled herself and turned to face the intruder.

There was an air about her which amounted to defiance. Of embarrassment there was not a trace. Her wide-open blue eyes met Tony's squarely; her trim little figure was taut with a sense of outrage and she made no secret of the fact that she was mad clear through.

"Well," asked Ivy Welch sharply, "are *we* intruding?"

The faintest ghost of a smile played about Tony's lips. These ultra-modern young things; so calm, so cool, so self-possessed, so supremely sure of themselves. Each crop of freshmen seemed to bring a new and earlier maturity. But Tony paid no attention to Ivy. She spoke to the man.

"Aren't you taking foolish chances, Pat?" she asked gravely.

He smiled and shrugged.

"Why does that interest you?"

"You know perfectly well why it interests me."

"Jealous?" he mocked.

Tony laughed. It was a short, bitter laugh and it stung.

"Of you?"

His face flushed. "You'd better run along, Tony," he advised, "and mind your own business."

"I shall. And I'll take Ivy with me."

The younger girl stared incredulously.

"Take me with you?" she echoed. "What are you talking about?"

"You'll understand some time, Ivy," said Tony gently. "If you'll just believe me now—"

Ivy stamped her foot impatiently.

"Don't be silly, Tony. I'm not a child."

"No-o. But you're only seventeen, and—"

"—And I'm getting older every day. Now listen here; I'm trying not to get sore. But my friends are nobody's business."

"Yes, they are. This time."

Ivy turned to Thayer.

"What's the big idea?" she demanded.

"Ask her," suggested Pat.

"It isn't a very big idea," said Tony. "And I can't explain, except to say that Pat understands what I'm driving at."

"Well, I don't," snapped Ivy. "I guess I'm a terrible dumbbell, and most likely I ought to be lying in a cradle playing with a rattle, but I can't get this at all—and I don't like it, either."

"I wish you'd believe—"

"I can't believe anything I don't even know. And if I choose to have a boy friend I can't see what affair it is of yours."

Tony Peyton shook her head. "I'm asking you to take my word that it would be best for you to keep away from Pat Thayer."

"Why? What's so terribly wrong with him? Or maybe you think I've never been kissed before. Is that it?"

"No. If it was any one else . . ."

"But it isn't, Tony. It's Pat. And I'm asking you why he's so dangerous. I'm trying to be nice, and it isn't very easy. The only thing I'll say is this: If you can't tell me what you're hinting at, then I'll stick with Pat as long as he wants."

Tony's eyes flickered to Thayer's sardonic face.

"Why don't you do the decent thing, Pat? Why don't you call it off?"

"Why should he?" inquired Ivy. Then she turned toward the man. "Tell me, Pat—what is there between you two?"

"Ask Tony," he repeated. "She'll tell you what she wishes you to know."

Jealously, Ivy faced Tony Peyton. She opened her lips to speak, and closed them again, for the expression she saw on the face of the slender senior flashed a message that whatever might exist between Tony and Pat Thayer— it certainly was not akin to love.

Tony was staring straight at Pat and there was no mistaking the loathing in her glance. The man himself seemed uncomfortable beneath her scrutiny and he tried to cover his embarrassment by assuming a highly superior air.

Tony's eyes didn't waver. She took him in from head to foot, and apparently found nothing attractive in his rather handsome face.

Paterson Thayer was an outstanding figure at Marland University. He had entered as a junior the preceding year, and this was his final senior semester.

He was twenty-three years of age. He was well over six feet in height; with a slim, well-muscled figure. He was distinctly a brunette and his manner was that of a man of the world.

Vague stories had trailed Pat to the Marland campus. Rumor had it that he had been invited to resign from the two Northern universities where he had done freshman and sophomore work. He hadn't been expelled exactly, but there were ugly stories having to do with certain social activities which conscientious Student Councils felt their colleges might well dispense with.

He had descended upon Marland as a handsome and exotic figure; one to fire the imagination of callow freshmen of the male sex and to excite a more than deep interest in the breasts of youthful co-eds.

For one thing, he had never been a part of Marland. He bore himself with a certain aloof dignity, as though the enthusiasms and excitements of college life were for those younger and less experienced than himself. He dressed immaculately and expensively, but disdained the extremes of tailoring so popular with the campus youth of the day. He had been elected to Psi Tau Theta at one of the other colleges and since arriving in the South had lived at the Psi Tau fraternity house.

Apparently he had ample money, and in the classroom he experienced little difficulty. The professors regarded him with a queer mixture of admiration and dislike. They felt that Pat Thayer was above the average student in worldly experience; they resented his superior manner and his insouciance, yet even those who detested him most heartily could not fail to give him excellent grades. He eased through his work with the same glorious indifference which so charmed the youngsters on the campus. He didn't exactly patronize the other students and yet he had become a traditional figure of wisdom—one who could draw from the well of his own experience to solve the problems of others.

His campus reputation was neither savory nor downright bad. Certain of the students spoke of him as a wild one, but no one had ever caught him in the act of being wild. "He's deep!" was the verdict—"Always pulling something and too wise to get caught at it." The result was that

he was the ruler at a court of youngsters who made hum-
ble obeisance to his superior wisdom and experience. He
was mature—yet it was a queer twist in the man's nature
that he had little contact with his classmates. They, too,
were beyond the callow years. They seemed to see him too
clearly for his own peace of mind, and so he contented
himself with the blind idolatry of freshmen and sophomores—immature, imaginative youths and girls who were
flattered by the friendship of this man of the world.

Tony knew him. She knew him more thoroughly than
any one else on the campus. She knew that he was arrogant
and weak and a poseur.

This affair with Ivy Welch! A kid! A plain, ordinary,
everyday, harmless little freshman flapper—and he had
turned her pretty blonde head with his courtliness; his air
of vast experience; his tremendous accumulation of years.

Tony liked Ivy Welch. She was wholesome and genuine—but, after all, she was only seventeen years of age,
and to seventeen the first amorous palpitations of the
heart are to be taken very seriously and not to be lightly
intruded upon.

As Ivy herself would have expressed it, Pat Thayer had
her running around in circles. She bitterly resented Tony
and didn't care how quickly Tony knew it.

"I still don't see where this is any of *your* business."

"It isn't—exactly. . . ."

"Then good-by. There's just room in the Bower for
two."

"Get this, Ivy—" Tony spoke rather more sharply than
she intended. "I don't give a hang what Pat Thayer does.
Right now I'm thinking of you."

"That's a laugh."

"I fancy," interrupted the man, "that she's really thinking about your brother—Larry."

Tony did not evade the challenge.

"Perhaps that's true, Pat."

"You see, Ivy," he said, "she figures that as a potential member of your family, it's up to her to protect innocent you from villainous me."

Ivy smiled with genuine amusement. "Can you beat it?" she inquired. "Can you even tie it? Say, listen, Tony—you don't really think I need protection, do you?"

"Yes."

"Oh! my God!"

"From Pat Thayer, at any rate."

"You know what, Tony? You give me a pain in the neck. And other places—inclusive. What's it all about?"

Tony flashed a glance at Pat. He was leaning against the trunk of a stalwart pine, obviously enjoying the scene hugely.

"He can explain," said Tony.

"I didn't ask him. I asked you."

"I'd rather not say anything."

Ivy stamped her foot. "You've got to say something. I have a right to know."

"What right?"

An incongruous sort of dignity settled about Ivy's girlish shoulders.

"Pat and I are engaged," she announced.

A light of genuine fear dawned in Tony's deep, black eyes. Her lips were without a smile; her expression stern and accusing. She spoke directly to Thayer, ignoring the girl.

"Have you really gone that far, Pat?

"You heard what Ivy said."

"I'm asking you."

"Yes—it's true."

Tony walked very close to him. "You've got to cut it!"

"Who says so?"

"I do."

"And what right have you to give orders?"

"I have plenty of right. You know I have, Pat Thayer. You've got to quit this thing and quit it quick. It was bad enough when I thought you were carrying on with a kid. But to let her think she's engaged to you . . ."

"Tony," broke in Ivy, and there was real distress in her voice, "I wish you'd tell me—"

"Oh! I could tell you plenty. This man is no good, Ivy. He's making a fool of you—"

Thayer's hand closed over Tony's arm.

"Lay off!" he growled. "I've stood about all I'm going to stand."

His manner was ugly and threatening, but Tony faced him defiantly, her cheeks blazing. "You've got me started, Pat—and I warn you I'll carry through if you don't call things off right here."

"You haven't the nerve."

"No? Try me and see."

"I shall. And get this, Tony: You can't bluff me. You've tried it before, and it don't work. Just one thing I'll warn you: Don't *you* start anything unless you're prepared to go through with it."

"I'll carry it through all right, Pat. I've stood a good deal, but I'm not going to tolerate this. For awhile I was sorry I butted in here. Now I'm glad. You've got this poor kid loco, and the sooner she knows what sort of rat you are, the sooner she'll come out of her trance."

His face was livid. Once again he grasped her arm.

"That's enough!"

"Take your hand away."

"Are you going to butt out of here—and stay out?"

"Not until you promise me to keep away from Ivy."

The man bent closer, until his face was on a level with Tony's. His gray eyes and her black ones clashed like drawn daggers. Ivy Welch, completely forgotten, stared at

them—not understanding what it was all about, but knowing that something very terrible was happening. There was
something between Pat Thayer and this girl; something
which her immature mind knew must be very tragic. She
felt like an outsider and dared not open her lips.

She had always been fond of Tony; had looked up to
her. But she loved Pat . . . even though she didn't like
his ugly expression, or the harsh sound of his voice, or
the manner in which he grabbed Tony's arm. It was a Pat
Thayer she had never before seen, and she felt vaguely
disturbed.

And finally Pat Thayer spoke, his words freighted with
fury.

"Up to now, Tony, I've played the game your way. So
long as you keep out of my affairs, I'll continue to play
it so. But if you want trouble, you'll have it—and plenty.
That's a warning."

"Will you do what I ask?" she inquired steadily.

"I'll do as I damn well please!"

Tony Peyton shook his hand from her arm. She stepped
back and surveyed the man. She was a slim, straight, militant little figure and her eyes blazed with anger and grim
determination.

"Very well," she said coldly, "that checks it right up to
me, doesn't it?"

"It does," he rasped. "And if I were you, I'd think twice
before I started anything."

Tony turned—and was gone without another word or
glance. Ivy Welch crept close to Thayer and slipped her
hand in his.

"Pat," she asked tremblingly, "what did she mean? What
is it all about?"

For an instant the man forgot himself.

"Hell!" he said nastily. "Forget it!"

CHAPTER III

Ivy drew back. For that instant she was a little girl again, rather than the mature woman she fondly believed herself to be. She was looking upon Pat Thayer with new and startled eyes.

The Bower was mottled with shadow as the sun, nearing its zenith, sent its rays trickling through the dense overhanging foliage. But the sweetness and softness had gone; a grim and sinister something had invaded the glade and Ivy was frightened.

Pat Thayer, cosmopolite, man of the world, expert in women—pulled himself together with a visible effort. The vicious, steely light fled from his cold gray eyes; his lips lost their sternness and he turned his attention once again to the exquisite little creature who had been swept from her feet by his mature suavity and charm. He smiled gently and slipped his arm about her yielding waist.

"Scared, Honey?"

The golden head nodded, and her voice came up to him.

"What did she mean, Pat?"

He was in control of his emotions now, and his light, bantering manner returned. It delighted Thayer to captivate women—even women so young and lacking in judgment as this child who snuggled against him.

"Sore," he announced.

"Jealous, you mean?"

"We-e-ell—maybe."

"But, Pat—I never thought Tony could act like that. I always thought she was kind of—of grown-up. You know: not the kind to get crazy mad like she did. It—it seemed that she was meaning a lot more than she said."

"Perhaps she was, Kid. She's a vindictive thing." His other arm crept about her pliant body and he drew her close against his breast. Her face turned up to his; eyes shining, lips parted with eagerness. "Kiss me, Rainbow."

She clung to him passionately. "Oh! I hated her, Pat. I thought that you and she—that is—you both—"

"Now, now, Sweetness. You're not going to mistrust your Pat that soon, are you? If some fool girl thinks she's got a claim on me . . ." He kissed her again, and she sighed and relaxed.

"We—we *are* engaged, aren't we, Pat?"

"Of course, Sugarplum. Firmly, finally and happily."

"And you're not peeved because I told Tony?"

"We-e-ell, we had decided that it better not be spread around the campus. But when the milk is already spilled—"

"I'm sorry, Sweetheart."

"And you won't doubt me any more?"

"No, Pat—never." But she pulled back in his embrace and stared up at him. "I couldn't help being jealous of Tony, though. I've always admired her and looked up to her—and all that. She's the most prominent girl on the campus—and the prettiest . . . and they say she's got just oodles of money."

He laughed shortly. "I guess Tony's no more of an icicle than lots of other girls. But she certainly is damn high-hat."

Ivy cuddled her hand in his big one. "I—I've never loved a man before this, Pat. And I guess no man knows just how a woman feels when another woman—especially a pretty one like Tony—who's got everything, and money and all—comes along like she did, and kind of— Oh! you know."

"Sure I know. But just so long as we understand each other . . ."

"I do understand you, don't I, Pat?"

"Nothing less."

"And you understand me?"

"I'll say so."

"And nothing is going to destroy our love? Oh! Pat—it's so different. I've run around with boys—just kids, you know. But I never thought I was in love with them. It's just kind of like I'd been saving myself always for you, if you know what I mean."

He looked down at her; his eyes narrowed to pinpoints, his body suddenly taut.

"I know, Honey. Now give me one more real kiss and we'll go."

Her arms were flung about his neck, and her half open lips pressed hotly against his. Her passionate idolatry pleased his overweening vanity. She appealed to his ego rather than to his heart. Secretly, he was merely amused. It was fun to win the worship of such a pretty girl, even if she was a silly kid. What mattered it to him if shortly he'd chuck her?

They pushed aside the screen of vines which guarded the entrance to the Bower and walked hand in hand through the glade. The bewitchment of a perfect May day had been dispelled by the unpleasant scene with Tony; but the air was warm and fragrant with the scent of new flowers; the little glen was filled with the song of birds, and from above—on the Hill—came the sound of an impromptu quartet singing not at all badly.

They followed the path to the top of the hill and gazed about the campus. Students sprawled under the trees. Off

to the side of Rogers Hall a half hundred cars were parked
and in most of them young couples sat intimately. The
spell of the season was upon the college. It was a day
for dreams and quietude and romantic reflection. They
strolled toward the Main Building, skirting the Bowl, and
just as they passed the tennis court some one joined them.

Maxwell Vernon was not happy. His short, pudgy figure
approached with quick, determined strides and he fancied
that he looked very dignified.

As a matter of fact it was difficult for Max to appear
dignified under any circumstances. He had a round little
body and a round, good-natured face. Even those who did
not know Maxwell, liked him. He had a quick smile for
everybody and not an enemy in the world. More than that,
he was supposed to be the wealthiest man on the campus.
He drove a big sport roadster and spent money frequently
and freely. He was friends with all the world: a carefree,
jolly, careless kid who, in some miraculous manner, had
managed to slip through three years at Marland and now
seemed almost ready to pass his final junior exams.

Most of the students laughed at Max—but they liked
him just the same. They called him a boob—but a darned
nice chap. There was always a song on his lips, and a smile.
He offered himself freely as the butt for jokes, and seemed
to enjoy being the victim of others' raillery. Innocuous,
light-hearted, living only in the present and totally un-
worried about the morrow, Max Vernon was as picturesque
in his own way as Pat Thayer was in his.

Between the two there existed a friendship which no
one even tried to understand. They seemed to have nothing in common and yet they were inseparable. Max idol-
ized Thayer. Thayer, on his part, openly derided Max . . .
and by doing so merely seemed to entrench himself more
firmly in Max's affections. Nor was that because Max
needed friends. The Marland campus was overflowing with

those who genuinely liked the sunny lad—and with those who pretended to like him because the strings of his purse were always open. Max liked to be popular and he paid for his popularity. He was weak . . . it was generally understood that one could make him do anything if one only approached him in the right way. It was not in him to choose a stony road when there was a smooth one handy— but for all this knowledge of his weakness and laziness, the campus loved him. He was Max Vernon—and as such was excused by students and faculty for many escapades which, in others, would have elicited censure.

But now as he approached Pat and Ivy, there was no smile on his moonlike face. Instead, it was set in stern lines and the high color in his cheeks told that he was not at all pleased. He nodded to Pat and addressed Ivy Welch.

"I guess this is nice," he said sharply. "Making a date with me and then standing me up for an hour."

She turned upon him a wide-eyed, baby stare.

"Why, Max," she exclaimed, "I never did!"

"I'll say you did."

"When?"

"Just now. Didn't you say you'd meet me at half-past ten? Didn't you?"

"Did I, Max?"

"You certainly did. And I don't like to be stood up, either. I guess if you don't want to keep a date with me you needn't make one."

Pat Thayer had been smiling superciliously. Now his sneering voice cut into the conversation.

"What you getting all heated up about, Max?"

"Plenty. Ivy had a date with me, and she didn't have any right standing me up."

"It wasn't her fault. I grabbed her and took her off for a walk."

"Yeh! But you didn't know she had a date with me."

"Didn't I?"

Vernon looked up quickly, his attention arrested by the
sneer.

"Did you?"

"Sure. She told me."

"You—you're just saying that to let Ivy down easy."

"I'm saying it because it's true. Who do you think you
are, Fat Boy, to say when a girl shall go with me and when
she shan't?"

"I know. . . . But, Pat! Ivy and I have been running
around together, and we had a date—"

"Oh! to thunder with your dates. If your girl prefers to
walk with me, she can do it."

Pat's manner puzzled Vernon. He was accustomed to
caustic comment from his older friend, but there was an
unpleasant, combative ring in Thayer's voice which roused
resentment even in the breast of the placid stout boy. He
knew nothing of the recent scene with Tony Peyton, he did
not know that Pat Thayer was in an ugly mood; but he did
know that while he would stand a very great deal from the
taller man—he would not tolerate the stealing of his girl.

Max Vernon was in the throes of a love affair with Ivy
Welch. True, Ivy had never seemed to requite his affection
to any startling degree, but Max was accustomed to that.
It seemed that all his life he had given of himself, humbly
asking nothing in return. And he had been doing very well
with Ivy until Pat Thayer commenced to take an interest
in her.

Pat was that way! It seemed as though he took a perverse delight in destroying Max's pleasure. Probably he
never would have noticed Ivy—she was such a kid!—had
it not been for Max's mad infatuation. Even now he was
sneering at the fat boy . . . never suspecting that Max
fancied himself very deeply and seriously in love with the
little blonde freshman.

Max turned on the girl.

"Are you coming with me now, Ivy?"

She tossed her head.

"Certainly not. You've acted silly, and—"

"I'll say he has!" interjected Thayer. "And how!"

Vernon's face flushed.

"You keep out of this, Pat."

"Who says I must?"

"I do."

"Well, I'll be dog-goned. *You* do! And who are you?"

In all their two years of intimacy, Thayer had never seen Max Vernon roused to anger. He was openly contemptuous of the younger man; did not even credit him with sufficient strength of character to become really angry. But he did not know that herein he was striking Vernon in his most vulnerable spot. He had opened a wound and was throwing salt into the hurt.

Max had stood a great deal from Pat Thayer. Their intimacy had been a peculiar one, and Max—had he thought evil of any one—could have told stories which would have corroborated a great many of the ugly rumors which were whispered about the campus anent Thayer.

Vernon had cut a great swath at Marland with his lavish wardrobe, his big, high-powered car, his brilliant parties and his free spending. But there were few who knew that Max had been more worried recently than he cared to admit even to himself. His money was gone, or nearly gone. Debt had piled up on him. He was an orphan, and the inheritance which had enabled him to spend so lavishly and which—to him—had seemed inexhaustible, was now nearly dissipated.

Loyally, Max had never permitted himself to think where a great deal of the money had journeyed. It was queer, though, that in two years of playing cards with Pat Thayer in the privacy of Pat's room there had been a steady flow of cash from Vernon to the older man. Like a good sport, Max put it all down to hard luck. That he had been scientifically and systematically bled by a college crook never occurred to him . . . or certainly it never had occurred until this moment when Thayer's manner betrayed to him a side of the man's character which ordinarily Vernon would have been too generous to discover.

As a matter of fact, Pat Thayer had lost interest in Vernon. Max was an insufferable bore. Pat had been interested so long as Max possessed money, but Thayer knew that he was broke. Well enough to burden himself with the friendship of a shallow youth so long as that youth possessed money which Thayer might acquire by means more reprehensible than doubtful. Now that there was no more golden flood to be had Thayer felt that the sooner he rid himself of Vernon's friendship, the quicker he'd be happy.

And so he sneered at Max before the girl with whom Max fancied himself in love. He taunted him . . . and, through sheer perversity, stole his girl.

Max was livid. For the first time in his life he was racked with a fierce, white anger.

"She's my girl," choked Max, "and you know it."

"Little boys don't have girls," grinned Thayer. "Do they, Ivy?"

Ivy was uncertain. Max was a child, of course, but she didn't want to hurt him.

"I didn't want to break that date, Max; but Pat asked me to take a walk with him—"

"And you went! I guess that shows me where I get off."

"I guess it does," snapped Thayer. "If you weren't so dumb you'd have found it out long ago."

"I'm not talking to you."

"Well, I'm talking to you. You're just a child. With less brains than most. I'm sick and tired of you . . . and I won't stand any more of this talk about who I shall walk with and when. Get that?"

"Careful, Pat."

"Of what?"

"Plenty." Vernon's roly-poly figure was trembling. "I don't want to have trouble with you."

"I'll say you don't. And I wish you'd quit your whining. If you were half a man you'd get out when another guy copped your girl."

"You mean—?"

"Ask Ivy. If she'd rather trot around with you, she's welcome. But I'm not going to share any girl with the college pest."

Max stared at Thayer. Then he looked at Ivy Welch. She was biting her lips. Queer how the tranquility of a perfect May day had twice been shattered by bitterness and quarreling. Ivy didn't understand what it was all about. She didn't understand the black mood which possessed Thayer—Pat, who was usually so suave and quiet and gentle. Nor had she ever seen Max Vernon angry. . . .

"I—I wish you boys wouldn't quarrel," she faltered.

"We're not quarreling," said Thayer. "I'm merely tired of Max's sniveling."

"But I thought you were friends."

"*Were* is right."

Max Vernon stepped close.

"You're kind of through with me, aren't you, Pat?"

"You said it."

"You've taken everything I had and now you're throwing me aside, eh?"

Pat cast a startled glance at Vernon. He had never credited Max with any such keenness of perception.

"Put it any way you like. Only for God's sake, quit whining around me."

"I'll quit, Pat. But I'll start thinking. I guess I've been awful dumb. You haven't. I begin to see more and more clearly that you've been wise as hell."

Pat Thayer raised his arm threateningly. "One more word like that, Vernon, and I'll—"

Max Vernon's eyes were half closed. He spoke in a grim whisper.

"If you lay a hand on me, Thayer," he said quietly, "I'll kill you!"

For a second the tableau held. Then—not knowing why he did so—Thayer lowered his fist. He turned away.

"Come along, Ivy," he said with a laugh which somehow was not hearty. "Let's get away from the kindergarten."

CHAPTER IV

Only the freshmen called Lawrence Shelby Welch "Professor." Sophomores, juniors and seniors who had shared undergraduate days with him called him Larry and no amount of faculty dignity could overcome the habit.

Larry Welch, Bachelor of Arts, Marland—1928, and candidate for a Master's degree, sat at his desk in Academic Hall facing rows of empty benches. The warm sunshine poured in through wide-flung windows. From the outside came the drone of a campus gone lazy, and Larry leaned back in his chair, half closed his eyes, and gave himself over to the luxury of formless—but delicious—thoughts.

One more month and he'd have his Master's degree. One more month and his connection with Marland would be officially severed. To-day of all days it came to Larry Welch most poignantly that he was sorry.

For five years his life had been lived on the Marland campus. Until the preceding June there had been showered upon him all the calcium glare that a great athlete and an outstanding student can receive in a small, intimate and prideful college.

He had started off as a star on all four freshman teams. The following year he was the great luminary of a fine football team, the flashing forward of a championship basketball quintet, a star sprinter on track and one of the greatest second basemen Marland had ever known or ever expected to know. He stood high in his classes; was a power in student activities; a regular fellow on a party; member of the exclusive Omega Gamma Nu fraternity and in his senior year had the unique distinction of captaining every athletic team in the school and of leading two of them to championships.

He was not a large man. At no time had Larry ever weighed more than a hundred and sixty-five. A casual observer would have considered him well formed, but rather inclined to slenderness; never suspecting the powerful muscular development beneath his loose-fitting clothes; nor the superb synchronization of those muscles with a keen and alert brain.

Nor was he handsome in a classic sense. Like his sister, Ivy, he was intensely blonde—rather Norse in type. His cheeks were pink and boyish; his eyes the blue of a spring sky. His manner inclined to slouchiness; he had a lazy, deliberate smile which lighted his whole face and he spoke with a soft, good-natured drawl.

Every person in college was Larry's friend, or wanted to be. The freshmen who took English from him this year adored him. There was a mad rush to take English VI and English VIII, his two courses. Frankly, he considered himself a rather poor teacher and was delighted that his freshmen liked him so well that they studied reasonably hard and did not confront him with the horror of flunking any one. He had put it to them straight at the beginning of the year—and they had responded as youngsters will when they are rightly approached. There wasn't a boy or girl of them who wouldn't—and didn't—work his head off for 'Fessor Welch.

But Commencement marked the end. To-day that idea struck Larry more forcibly than ever before. While the weather was bleak and damp, Commencement had seemed far away; now that summer had burst suddenly upon the campus, it seemed that the end was upon him. He almost regretted his refusal of an offer from the President that would carry with it the position of assistant football coach and associate professor. Yet he knew that he dared not let sentiment sway him. He gazed clear-eyed into the future and knew that he must start building immediately.

He was now twenty-three years of age. In the city of Birmingham—some forty miles away—a good job awaited him; a job offering him enough salary to live well, save a trifle—and plan for the future; the last being something which Larry most ardently desired to do.

The future . . . the prospect was delightfully linked with visions of a home and a girl . . . a girl slim and straight and vividly brunette; a girl whom he had known for three marvelous years and who was the envy of Marland if for no other reason than that she had won the affection of the great Larry Welch.

And even as Larry thought of her, the door opened and Tony Peyton entered the room abruptly.

Larry turned, and for a moment did not move. She stood framed in the doorway, an exquisite little figure, her big, black eyes shining into his, an eager smile on her sensitive lips. He gazed his idolatry for the full period of time it took the mellow chimes of the old clock in the tower of the Main Building to toll twelve. Noon! Noon of May Day!

It was the girl who broke the spell. She closed the door leading into the corridor and advanced toward his desk. He was smiling eagerly as he rose to greet her.

"Believe it or not," he challenged: "I was just thinking of you, Tony."

She flushed at the declaration in his eyes. She put both her hands in his and he pressed them tightly.

"I wish I loved you less, Tony."

"Why?"

"I'd kiss you."

For an instant the roguish smile which he so loved played across her lips. But it was gone almost as soon as it appeared and the face she turned up to his was very, very serious.

"Have you a class this hour, Larry?"

"No."

"Where can we talk?"

"Here. Nobody's likely to bother us—in a classroom on such a day as this. He took her chin in his hand and turned her head this way and that, regarding her quizzically. "Why the misery?"

She shook her head and seated herself on one of the benches.

"Sit next to me, Larry. I want to have you close when I talk—without the necessity of looking straight at you."

"Sweet suffering tomatoes! I never had that one pulled before."

"I'm serious—I mean I want to talk seriously."

"Oh, shuh! Tony—this is no day for melancholy. Forget what's eating you and let's thresh it out to-morrow. What say?"

"I can't, Larry. It's on my chest and I've got to get it off."

"But not now. Let's grab my flivver and take the air for an hour. Lord knows no healthy person has the right to stay indoors on this sort of a day."

She pressed his hand. "Trying to snap me out of it, aren't you, Larry? Good scout! But it's no go. We're in for a talk—"

He settled himself beside her. "Fire when ready. But there's nothing in the world to justify such seriousness."

"Yes, there is. Plenty."

"Convince me. If it's anything about this job they've offered me here—"

"It isn't, Larry. It isn't about you at all."

"No-o. . . ." He glanced at her out of the corners of his eyes and felt a premonition of trouble. This wasn't the Tony he knew. Usually she had a laugh on her lips; was ready with quick repartee . . . seemed to look upon life with a smile. But now the cameo face was set in lines which bordered on sternness: Larry received the impression that she was older than himself—a thing manifestly absurd. There was trouble reflected in those fine eyes. . . . Her first words, which came hesitatingly, bore out his fear.

"Something's wrong, Larry; awfully wrong. I've got to talk it out with you."

He fell in with her mood. "All right, Tony. Let's have it. You know dog-gone well if there's anything I can do—"

"I know. That's why I came to you. At any rate, it's one of the reasons."

"And the other?"

"Because . . ." She hesitated, then took the plunge bravely. "Well, it's about Ivy."

He straightened. "My sister?"

She nodded, and something in her manner caused a look of worry to dawn in his own eyes. Not even Tony quite fathomed the depth of affection which existed between Larry Welch and his sister. Here on the campus he felt like a father to her; with all a father's inordinate pride.

"What about Ivy?"

Tony turned in her seat until she faced Larry directly.

"I can talk straight, can't I?"

"You know you can. As a matter of fact, I've never known you to do anything else. You've got me a trifle scared."

"I want to," she said simply.

"Ivy's in trouble?"

"Yes . . . and no. That is, Larry, she isn't now—but she may be, unless something is done. I'm mixed up in it, too.

You'll most likely hear from Ivy about it . . . and I thought
I'd better come to you first."

For the moment his thoughts were all of the kid sister
whom he adored.

"What's wrong, Tony?"

She met his eyes levelly.

"How do you like Pat Thayer?"

He hesitated, and shook his head. "Not particularly,"
he admitted, "but that doesn't mean anything."

"He isn't the sort of man you'd pick for Ivy, is he?"

"No-o. Not if I were doing the picking."

"Well—Ivy is in love with him!"

"With Pat Thayer?"

"Yes. And she thinks she is engaged to him."

He took Tony's arm and leaned close. "Is that what has
been worrying you, Tony? Is that what you came here to
see me about?"

"Yes. . . ."

And quite suddenly he threw back his head and laughed.
He laughed softly, but with tremendous relief.

"Gosh! What a goose you are! And what if she is nuts
about Thayer? Ivy's nobody's fool. She can take care of
herself."

Tony bit her lip. She spoke in a hard little voice. "You
refuse to worry about it, Larry?"

"Sure, I do. Even my sister has got to cut her eyeteeth
some time, and so—"

The color drained from the girl's cheeks.

"I'm afraid, then," she said in a hard little voice, "that
I've got to tell you more than I intended."

CHAPTER V

She hesitated, but only for a second. Then, without looking at her companion, she told of the scene in the Bower—
of Pat Thayer and Ivy Welch, of her intrusion and of the
bitterness which had followed. Larry listened attentively,
reserving comment. He was more worried about Tony than
about his sister. This wasn't the Tony he knew. She was not
customarily prone to exaggerate or theatricalize. Yet he
sensed that there was a great deal yet to be told.

"You're worried about Ivy?" he asked when she had finished.

"Yes."

"Because Pat Thayer doesn't seem to be the right sort
of fellow?"

"It's because I know he isn't."

He shook his head and a slow, tolerant smile played
about his lips.

"If it had been some other kid, Tony—would you have
become so excited?"

She struggled to be honest. "Perhaps not, Larry. But I'd
have warned her."

"I'm afraid you're not fair to Thayer," he said. "We
understand, of course, that ugly rumors followed him to
Marland. But nothing was ever substantiated. He was a

member of Psi Tau Theta when he came here . . . and that speaks pretty well for him. He is obviously a gentleman—"

"Outwardly—yes."

"That's about all one sees casually, isn't it? Now listen, Tony: I'm going to be honest with you. I think you've gone off the deep end. We're friends and Ivy is my sister. You forget that she's a kid girl just like any one of a hundred other freshmen co-eds. Perhaps it's better that she picked a man like Pat Thayer for her first love affair. I reckon every girl has to go through that once—an infatuation for a man older than herself. I'll admit frankly that I don't like the man much better than you do. But we don't know anything against him, and—"

"How has he been living since he came to Marland?" she questioned abruptly.

Larry frowned. "You mean the Max Vernon thing?"

"Exactly. It's common knowledge, Larry, that Thayer has bled Vernon of every cent he had. They've played cards for big money . . . and Max has lost. Have you watched that kid in the past few months? Up to last fall you never saw him that he wasn't grinning. He didn't have a care or worry on earth. But now . . . he's older, and he's serious. Every one knows that he's broke. Why, Larry, they say that he's run through more than seventy-five thousand since he's been at Marland and that Pat Thayer has most of it."

"Isn't that Vernon's lookout? If he's a bum gambler and chooses to press his bad luck—"

"A man can't always win honestly, can he?"

"Perhaps not. But you're accepting rumor as fact. We don't know that Pat has been trimming Vernon."

"Trimming! Stealing his money, you mean. Of course, we don't know it. But the whole college is pretty sure. And now he's gone out after Ivy. He seems to take a perverse delight in making Vernon miserable now that he's got his money. Max is crazy about Ivy."

"Sure he is. And he's a nice kid. But I've got no right to tell my sister whom she shall run with. She's got a good head on her shoulders, Tony; a darned good head. I'm fond of her and I think she likes me pretty well. But she wouldn't stand for it a minute if I chased after her telling her what she must and mustn't do. Now listen—" He faced her once again and took one of her hands in his: "Something has run off with your nanny. You've magnified nothing into something terrible . . . and you're all wrong. I don't hold any brief for Thayer, but I do say that until we know something we have no right to butt into his relationships with any girl on the campus—even if that girl is Ivy. Let's forget it, Tony. I appreciate the way you feel, but if you'll sleep over it a bit, you'll see that you're exaggerating the thing and being darned unfair to Thayer."

Tony rose and walked to the window. Her figure was outlined in the brilliant sunlight and Larry Welch stared at her curiously. Here was a girl he didn't know at all; a girl gripped by a resentment which he could not understand.

Tony looked out across the campus. Her eyes dwelt on the groups of students lounging under the trees; she followed three or four couples as they walked slowly from the classrooms toward the Students' Activities Building for their cafeteria lunch. It was all so peaceful and quiet; the stage was so magnificently set for gentle romance untinctured by grimness. And yet . . .

Oh! Larry was right not to understand. He was a generous person who had the faculty of looking at things through the other fellow's eyes. She knew that he didn't like Thayer, either; that he rather resented the tall man's flamboyant display of superiority; his flagrant cosmopolitanism. It was equally certain that Larry could not be incited to action by mere conjecture or rumor. Tony Peyton left the window suddenly and returned to Larry. She stood before him, slim and determined, and something in her manner caused him to rise from his seat. They stood facing one another: the blond young man and the vividly beautiful girl . . . but now they had the seriousness of supreme maturity.

She faced him with rare courage. He waited for her to speak, his face grave. And when she did, her words startled him.

"Larry," she said in a voice little above a whisper, "you've often told me that you love me. Do you?"

His face flamed and, impulsively, his arms went out toward her . . . then dropped again. But if he was successful in controlling a gesture, he was less so in keeping a tremble from his voice.

"I love you, Tony."

She looked up at him. There was no sign of color in her cheeks.

"I will tell you something I have never said before, Larry. I love you. . . . No!" as he impulsively stepped close to her. "Don't touch me—please! Not now. I'm not finished."

"But you do love me . . .?"

"Yes. I wonder that you haven't known it. I wonder that you haven't seen it in every look and word that has passed between us. You have; haven't you?"

"I have hoped," he said humbly. "But when one cares for a girl as I do for you, dear. . . ."

"I understand," she said, with a sudden rush of tenderness. "I do—really."

"Is—is it because you—do care, Tony, that you've worried about Ivy?"

"Yes. And it's more than that." She made a helpless little gesture. "You see, Larry—I had hoped to get you to put a stop to the affair without forcing me to say what I have to. There is something I didn't want to tell you—"

"Don't you tell me a thing you don't want, Tony."

A wistful little smile played fitfully about her lips.

"This time I have to. Perhaps I'm glad. . . . I guess I've sounded rather ridiculous and catty. I've apparently made a mountain out of a molehill. I shouldn't wonder but that you're somewhat disgusted with me."

He laughed shakily. "I'm only thinking of one thing . . . what you just told me."

"I'm thinking of that, too, Larry. I haven't thought about anything else for a long, long time."

She stopped talking. Her hands were tightly clasped. Then she stepped very close and looked levelly into his eyes.

"You've known for a long time that I loved you, Larry. I know I've never said it in so many words, but you've known it just the same. Have you ever wondered, dear, why—loving you—I would never consent to marry you?"

He shook his head slowly.

"I've never dared wonder that far, Tony. I've been too busy wondering—and worrying—about whether you cared."

"I do care. You know it now. And yet, saying that—I tell you in the same breath that I can't marry you. Now do you wonder why?"

"Yes," he answered quietly, "I do."

For a long time she did not speak. She felt like a woman about to plunge from a great height. Her body was tense and cold. Then she told him—with a rush of words which hurt and which required sheer physical courage.

"Larry," she said steadily, "the reason I cannot marry you is because Pat Thayer is my husband!"

CHAPTER VI

An expression of utter bewilderment crossed Larry's face. He understood the girl's words without being able immediately to grasp their significance.

His mind leaped off on a queer tangent. He recalled a day on the gridiron when, playing without a headguard, he had been slammed to the ground and knocked into that hazy condition which is technically described as "goofy." He didn't know what happened immediately afterward except that he was not conscious of pain and the whole stadium seemed bathed in a gentle glow. His only feeling was one of comfortable well-being. But they told him afterwards that he had been walking around in circles— and doing that rather unsteadily—until a hardhearted coach had ended the gossamer dreams by dashing half a bucket of ice water into his face.

Larry remembered that sensation very clearly: the sudden snapping back into agonized consciousness; the hammering pain in his head—a pain which seemed to extend downward through every muscle in his body. He blinked and suffered acutely—but his brain was clear and he was prepared to play the game again.

It all came back to him now as he stared at Tony Peyton. He had been in a delicious haze and her words had struck him with the same cruel force as that bucket of cold water. They clarified his thoughts . . . but they hurt. They hurt a great deal. They left him stunned . . . but grim. He didn't—even yet—grasp the full portent—but he felt a new and painful injury, and realized that he must carry on toward some vague goal.

And then he understood more poignantly than ever before just how much he loved this slender, level-eyed girl. His blue eyes sought her black ones to exchange a message of frank and unashamed love. Then it seemed that a sinister shadow came between them—a shadow very real to any man and woman in a like situation, but starkly tragic to persons as young and filled with the passion of life as these two. Pat Thayer's wife! The word, so delicately delightful when considered in conjunction with himself, now struck him unpleasantly. She belonged to Thayer. She was married to the man about whose commanding and exotic and highly unpleasant personality there existed unsavory rumors. It was amazing that the campus had not learned of this.

Tony looked at him compassionately. She suffered because she had hurt him, yet she felt a sense of infinite relief that she had elected to share her burden. It had been a noxious secret. She had despised herself. . . . She saw Larry's blond head move slowly from side to side as though he were struggling to understand what it meant; striving to peer into the future and reconstruct his dreams. The girl took his hand in both of hers and gazed straight into his eyes.

"I'm married to Pat," she said quietly, and her cheeks were crimson; "but I've never been his wife."

He drew in his breath sharply. "You—you mean, Tony—"

"Just that, Larry. There has never been anything between Pat and myself except a ceremony."

A great load lifted from the heart of the young man. He dared a question.

"Do you love him?"

Her eyes widened.

"I despise him."

And young Mr. Welch threw back his head and smiled.
"Gosh!" he said. "That makes me happy. When you told
me he was your husband I felt sick all over. Now, it doesn't
seem important. Not a bit. Oh! I know I'm silly, but it
seems as though anything can be adjusted if it's true that
you hate him."

"It's true all right enough." Then she lowered her voice.
"Can't you understand now why I worried for Ivy when I
saw her in his arms? Don't you see how different it is? I
happened to know that Pat Thayer is legally married. That
being the case, it isn't exactly fair to Ivy to permit the
thing to continue, is it?"

"Scarcely." A new and square set came to his jaw. "I'll
have to fix things. . . . I sure will." He was silent for a moment, then seated himself again. "Sit down, Tony."

She was glad enough to obey. She felt the strain of the
past few minutes. She was glad when he took her hand and
spoke in a gentle, understanding voice.

"Can you tell me all about it, Tony?"

She nodded.

"When did it happen?"

She answered without turning.

"Last year—November, 1927."

"Where?"

"Nashville. When the team went up to play Vanderbilt."

"I see. . . . You hadn't known Thayer very long then."

"No. He had only been in college two months. The
whole campus was wild about him. He was a unique sort
of figure, and rather impressive. I was a year and a half
younger then than I am now. From the day he arrived at
Marland the girls were all crazy about him. He seemed to
have singled me out for his particular attention—"

"I remember," said Larry grimly. "I sure do!"

"I was flattered. I ran around with him a good deal. He took me to lots of dances. . . . I wasn't with you much then, Larry. You were on the team and Coach had you training pretty hard and you were always making up classes you had missed on football trips. Anyway, I was just a silly kid. That's why I know how Ivy feels right now . . . she regards Pat Thayer pretty much as I did for awhile; not in love with him nearly so much as she's dazzled by his manner and experience.

"Anyway, I know I was flattered because the most picturesque man on the campus had chosen me. I liked to be with him . . . and for a while I was fond of him. He can be pretty charming if he wants to. He's not like most of the boys. I was at the precise age to which maturity appeals. I regarded most of the students as kids, and looked on Pat as a full-grown man in spite of the fact that he was a classmate. Looking back on it, I know it was a kid infatuation with no more depth than the water in a goldfish bowl."

Her voice trailed off, and when he did not speak, she continued.

"I'm trying very hard to make you see through my eyes as they were then, Larry; trying to make you understand me as I was, rather than as I am. What the Antoinette Peyton of November, 1927, did would be impossible for the Tony of May, 1929. Do you understand?"

"Sure. Go ahead."

She drew a long breath.

"The girls all envied me. I was silly enough to let my head get turned by that, too. See, I'm not sparing myself at all. And then came the game with Vandy. Pretty near all the student body went to that. I went. And so did Pat.

"You don't know much about that day, Larry, because you were with the team all the time. But we descended on Nashville and took it by storm. Our band in new uniforms;

a parade through the downtown section . . . I forgot that I was a dignified junior and did things which only freshmen are supposed to do.

"I went to the game with Pat, and you remember what happened there. Our last minute rally that tied the score. Marland had tied one of the greatest teams in the Southern Conference . . . and done it for the first time in history. It was an intoxication. Everything was wonderful . . . and now you can get ready to laugh at me. Now you're going to learn what an idiot I am."

"Well," he prompted: "What?"

"Pat Thayer proposed to me during the last five minutes of that football game, Larry. He kept insisting that Marland was going to tie the score and I kept saying that we weren't—trying to bring us good luck by talking like a jinx. 'I'll bet we tie or win,' said Pat. 'We won't!' I answered. 'I know we haven't a chance.' 'You're not game to bet,' he taunted. Of course I said I was. Then he leaned so close that nobody else could hear and whispered to me: 'Let's see how game you are, Tony. If Marland gets as good as a tie out of this, you're to marry me right after the game.' 'Don't be silly,' I said, and he insisted that he was serious. 'And you'd better say yes quick, Tony—or I'll jinx the whole team.'"

She looked away, and there was a tremor in her voice.

"You can't understand it now, Larry. There's no use trying to make you understand."

"I do, though."

"You don't! You can't! It isn't possible—sitting here in your classroom, looking over a period of eighteen months and trying to make a person understand how a kid girl could get drunk with football excitement and plunge into a serious thing like marriage. It isn't sane. And it isn't reasonable to expect you to understand something which I myself can't fathom now."

"Just the same," he said gently, "I do understand."

"I hope so. . . . Anyway, I made the bet. You know what happened after that. Slick Robinson broke away for that long run. You and Eddie Farrell were running interference. We tied the score. Everybody went crazy. Then the game ended and Pat and I drifted out with the crowd. And once we got outside and into a taxi, Pat announced that we were going straight to the Court House and get a license. At first I thought he was joking, then I saw he was serious. I laughed at him, and he accused me of being a bad sport.

"I can pretty well summarize what happened then. I tried every way in the world to argue him out of it. He was gentle and considerate—and firm. He kept talking about paying my debt . . . and you can imagine how that struck me. Besides, I liked him. I was infatuated, if you want the truth. The excitement of the game had thrown me off balance. I retained enough sanity to strike a bargain with him. I said I'd go through with it if he'd be willing to keep the marriage a secret—and merely a ceremony—until vacation time. I promised him we'd take a honeymoon in the summer if he'd do what I wanted. He protested, but finally agreed. . . ."

She stopped talking. Larry gazed intently at her averted face.

"And then, Tony?"

"And then," she responded, without turning, "we were married."

CHAPTER VII

Everything seemed to be summed up in her simple statement. She spread her arms helplessly, and the young man
stared at her.

The sun which streamed in through the window played
on her thick, bobbed hair. It limned the delicate profile
and clung caressingly to her figure. Larry Welch was queerly elated—although he told himself fiercely that he was a
fool for feeling that way. But somehow he couldn't be depressed when he remembered that she had turned to him
for help and that she had given him her confidence. What
amazed him most, however, was the fact that the marriage
successfully had been kept secret.

"I had hoped not to tell you"—she was speaking in
a soft, tired voice—"until after we should have been
divorced or had the marriage annulled. I detested the idea
of a campus scandal—or gossip—or whatever it would
have been. I was waiting until graduation. Then I was going west or to France or somewhere and quietly have the
whole miserable affair ended. But seeing Ivy—with him—
that rather changed things about, Larry."

"I understand. I wish you had told me before, though."

"I couldn't. I felt ashamed. Degraded. I didn't want any
one to know. It wouldn't have been pleasant if the campus
had discovered. Things would have been different if I had

been living with Pat. But to be married and separated—to
be at tending the same classes and the same dances, to
have every one know that we were husband and wife and
yet were having nothing to do with each other . . . that
wouldn't have been nice."

"I agree with you. And, going back to the beginning . . .
what caused you to—to become un-infatuated?"

She gave a little smile of distaste. "Several things, Larry.
You see, when I told you about Ivy I insisted that I knew
a good deal about Pat Thayer. You thought I was unfair—
accepting ugly truth. I still don't know how true those
rumors are, but I do know that there isn't a decent bone in
Paterson Thayer's body."

She turned toward Welch now, and spoke with fierce
intensity.

"I'll talk frankly, Larry—because it is your right to
know. Before we were married, Pat and I agreed that the
marriage was to be a mere form until summer. We were
to be good friends, just as we had been since he came to
Marland—but that was all. It wasn't long after the ceremony that he made it clear that he didn't intend to keep
the bargain."

Her cheeks were flushed and Larry's were dead white.

"No need to go into detail. It wasn't very pleasant. And
the matter wasn't adjusted immediately. I didn't regard
myself as his wife and told him so. He was rather nasty
about it. One thing led to another . . . and then we had
our first quarrel." She gave a short, bitter laugh. "One
can find out a good many things about a man when he is
thoroughly angry. I found out about Pat Thayer then. He
wasn't the suave, courteous gentleman that I had known.
Before we had finished I told him that he might have saved
himself the trouble of going through with a marriage ceremony. I told him I intended to get a divorce immediately,

and then, Larry, was when the cloven hoof became unmistakably visible.

"He refused to consider a divorce. I had married him with my eyes open. He didn't intend that I should have any grounds for divorce. And if I cared to bring action, he'd fight it in such a way that the Marland campus would become a thoroughly uncomfortable place.

"I hated that idea, Larry. I love Marland. I wanted my degree from here. But much as I wanted to see it through then . . . I don't believe I could have stayed on here if there had been a rotten annulment action with half the students gossiping and wondering, and Pat Thayer testifying God knows what when the case came to be heard. You see, he let me understand that he would not be limited by the truth should the case come to trial."

She rose and crossed to the window, then returned to the seat by Welch's side.

"Ever since that day, Larry—I've felt unclean. If it didn't sound like cheap drama I'd say that I became a woman overnight. My whole perspective changed. I stalled him off, and was surprised that he seemed content to wait. There was no mistaking the feeling between us. I hated him, and he came to hate me even more thoroughly. Then— one day—he came to me and asked the loan of a large sum of money!"

"Good Lord! You don't mean . . ."

"Precisely. Blackmail. I refused and he threatened to spread around the campus the story I had been trying to keep secret. No divorce, mind you, no annulment. He intended to insinuate . . . to let the student body form its own opinions. I called him a blackmailer, and he cheerfully admitted that he was. He asked me furthermore what I intended to do about it. He said I'd never miss the amount he wished to borrow—which was true—and, anyway, I

loaned it to him. In the months that followed I loaned
him more money, Larry—just to keep his filthy mouth
shut. And it isn't the amount. I can afford to spend a
good deal more than I've given him. But it was terrible to
feel that I was being bled by a man whose name I legally
bore. Time after time I determined to end it by suing for
an annulment. Then I'd think about the embarrassment
of staying on at Marland after the gossip became general—and I wasn't brave enough. I determined to make the
best of a rotten bad bargain. I knew that he had worked
me scientifically. He had singled me out as a wealthy girl.
He had found the catch easier than he anticipated—that
was all. It was my plan to wait until after I had my degree
. . . then to end the affair legally. Of course my friends
would know, but I wouldn't be thrown in daily contact
with him, or with them." She paused for a moment, then
turned impulsively toward the young man. "I wonder if
you understand?"

"Of course I do, dear."

"And you think I was cowardly?"

"Not a bit. I think you've been rather fine about it."

She noticed his manner of talking: there was nothing
soft or gentle in his voice. His teeth were tight set and his
big fists were clenched. It was obvious that he was making
a distinct effort to keep himself under control.

"A pretty nasty mess all 'round," he commented at
length. "Just plain rotten."

She nodded. "You understand why I hesitated to tell—
even you?"

"Yes." Suddenly he turned to her and she saw that his
cheeks were dead white. "Damn it! Tony—I'm trying to
keep a rein on myself. It isn't an easy job."

She was surprised. It was the first time in the four years
she had known him that she had ever seen him gripped

by anger. She had seen him on the football field: a flashing, fighting demon . . . but always with a good-natured friendly smile on his lips; always with a word of congratulation for the other fellow. Now he was different. There was something primitive in the ugly set of his lips and the blue of his eyes had changed to an icy gray.

"I've kept pretty quiet, Tony," he said, choosing his words with meticulous care. "I've tried not to let it get my goat. At first I was all with Pat. Goodness knows I'd be the last one to blame him for wanting to marry you. I even"— he hesitated for the briefest fraction of an instant, and his cheeks flushed—"I even didn't blame him when you told me that he wasn't awfully keen about keeping his part of the bargain . . . about—about waiting until summer for a honeymoon.

"But the rest of it . . . it's pretty rotten. That any man should have married you because you have a little money; that he should have blackmailed you for two years; that he should have been—well, nasty in his attitude toward you. That hits me pretty hard, Tony; perhaps because I care for you so much.

"Then there's Ivy. I was fair to him about that. Ivy's a nice kid, and pretty—even if she is my sister. If he wanted to flirt with her—that was their business. But if he's a married man—and that kind of a man . . ." He rose abruptly. "I'm going to have a pretty straight talk with Mr. Paterson Thayer. A pretty damn straight talk."

"No!" She was on her feet and her hand was on his arm. This new Larry frightened her. "You're in no mood to talk to him—"

He laughed harshly. "Don't worry about me."

"It isn't that, Larry. But can't you see that you mustn't clash with Pat? He'd be liable to get nasty and spread the story."

"He won't," prophesied Larry grimly. "I can promise that."

"You mustn't go to him now."

"I've got to. Leave yourself out of it, if you wish. I've got to consider Ivy. His affair with her can't be permitted to run on."

"That's true," she said thoughtfully. Then an idea came to her and she looked up brightly. "Let's compromise, Larry."

"How?"

"You go chat with Ivy. See if you can do anything with her. Of course she mustn't know that I'm Pat's wife. But see if you can't get her to do what you want—to stay away from Pat. And meanwhile I'll go to Pat right now. I'll tell him that if he continues running around with Ivy I'll tell the truth to the whole campus. That will spike his guns. Don't you see that's the sensible thing?"

He looked at her keenly.

"Do you think you can bluff him, Tony?"

She seemed taller than her height and older than her years.

"This time, Larry," she said, "I'll make him understand that I'm not bluffing."

CHAPTER VIII

The Main Building of Marland University looks down from the top of a modest hill upon the quiet, far-flung residential town of Marland. It has long been a subject for argument on the Marland campus as to which side of Old Main was intended by its architects as the front.

One large door opens on the campus and gives a view of the Bowl and the college buildings on either side. The other terminus of the hall which traverses Old Main ends in a flight of five stone steps which, in turn, marks the beginning of a long straight road which drops downward for the distance of two city blocks to a main east-and-west traffic artery. Citizens of Marland regard this as the front of the building. Students, for the most part, regard as the front that side of the building which can be seen from the campus itself.

The roadway which descends somewhat precipitously from the Main Building to Marland Road is lined on both sides with fraternity houses. These houses are of various vintages and sizes. There are the old ones—some stately and some merely houses—and the new ones which are, in the majority, constructed of red brick and white stone and built pretty much to a pattern.

Halfway down the hill stands the home of Psi Tau Theta, by all odds the largest of them all. By the same token, it is the least modern; a huge, rambling, wooden affair of mellow years and pleasing contour. It is three stories in height and the front of its first floor is spanned by a capacious veranda which is the pride and delight of all Psi Tau's.

On either side of this fraternity house can be found modern structures: pretty in an unimaginative way. To the right is the home of Omega Gamma Nu and on the left the building which affords sanctuary to the young gentlemen of Lambda Beta Pi. From across the street the ugly bulk of the Rho Tau Sigma house leers enviously at the three aristocrats, while up as far as the Main Building and down to Marland Road are the other fraternity homes. The street has a name, but no one at Marland knows what it is. Since the days when the first house was constructed on that street, it has been known as Fraternity Row, and will continue to be known by that title so long as there is a University.

Old as it is, Psi Tau Theta dominates the Row. It has a quiet dignity which the other houses lack; the sort of superior aloofness which marks the façade of an exclusive city club. Its members are not at all averse to sprawling in the hammocks which infest the huge veranda—where they may be seen and envied by passing students. They have a very pardonable pride in their fraternity.

Shortly after noon of May first—at the very hour when Tony Peyton and Larry Welch were having their conversation in Larry's classroom—two young men descended the hill, turned in at the Psi Tau Theta house, flung their notebooks disdainfully on a porch table and sought accommodation: one in a saggy hammock and the other in a somewhat decrepit wicker chair.

The lad who flopped in the hammock was Rube Farnum, a tall, angular, gangly junior whose nickname fitted his appearance rather more snugly than his background.

Actually Rube was an urban product. He wore ill-fitting clothes with easy indifference; he had a thin face and a huge mouth which could—and invariably did—expand alarmingly into an infectious smile. He took nothing in the world seriously, unless it was his membership in Psi Tau Theta.

Phil Gleason, his companion, was superbly antithetic. Phil was also a junior; but even in the first hot wave of approaching summer, he was immaculate—jaunty, even. He was short and slender and inclined to be dynamic. He spoke always in explosives, whereas nothing ever excited Rube to more than a slow, amused drawl.

They gave themselves over now to an idle discussion of nothing whatever. They exchanged words, rather than ideas. The weather was exerting a somnolent effect and such conversation as they maintained was fragmentary and effortless.

Fraternity Row was peopled with students who moved slowly down the hill, or even more slowly in the opposite direction. The verandas of the various fraternity houses were not empty nor were they particularly well filled. On several of the porches, young men slept calmly in hammocks. A few were reading. But mostly the occupants of the porches had given themselves over to the sensuous delights of the day and were frankly just simply sitting.

Phil Gleason glanced at his watch; frowned, shook the timepiece violently, and then turned to his friend.

"Damn thing's busted again!" he exploded. "What time, Rube?"

Mr. Farnum did not hasten. With a leisurely, utterly languid gesture he reached into his pocket and extracted a large but reliable watch.

"Twelve-thirty," he remarked as he replaced the watch and relaxed again into a condition of glorious desuetude.

"Hmph! I got a class at one-twenty. No sense to classes in this kind of weather."

"Ain't a lot of sense to 'em anyway," observed Rube—
"for a guy like you."

"Wise-cracking, eh? I guess you're a shining light."

"We-e-ell, they never dropped me off the basketball
squad because I was dumb in classes."

"Sure not! You never could make the squad. You're too
confoundedly lazy." Gleason's sharp eyes swung toward the
street as a tall, graceful figure turned in on the concrete
walk leading to the house. "Hello!" he observed softly—
"Here comes What the Well-Dressed Man Should Wear."

Rube eyed the approaching figure of Pat Thayer with
tolerant amusement. "Golly!" said he—"I wish I was a raw
freshie so I could get a kick out of just looking at that
bird. Ain't he too sweet?"

Thayer, happily ignorant of their caustic comment,
mounted the porch steps and nodded to the occupants of
chair and hammock.

"Hello, Phil. Howdy, Rube."

"'Lo, Pat."

Thayer made one more casual remark as he passed
through the door into the big downstairs reception hall.
"Working hard, I see."

Once he had gone they looked at each other. Rube Farnum's big mouth twisted into a grimace of distaste. "Pat
Thayer is always saying things I'd like to hear from somebody else," he said. "And I get sore when he says 'em."

"Swine!" snapped Gleason.

"Who? Me?"

"Right now I'm speaking of him."

"Thanks." Rube chuckled. "But he's got it soft, that
bimbo. Star boarder here. Ever been in that room of his?"

"Yeh. Second floor, front. Bay window and everything.
Fixed up like a boudoir of one of Louis Fourteenth's lady
friends. Not a pennant. Not a pillow. He's so dam' proud
of the fact that he ain't collegiate."

"Ain't it so? And if—" Rube cocked his head on one side and listened attentively. Not that there was any necessity for close attention, for the soft summer air was rudely shattered by the roaring of a high-powered motor which thundered to the world that its muffler had been cut out. "I think," said Rube, "that our most shrinking violet is about to approach in his gasoline chariot."

They looked down the hill in time to see a long, low gray touring car, of heavy and expensive type, swing violently into Fraternity Row from Marland Road. It roared proudly up the hill, slewed abruptly in front of the Psi Tau Theta house and jerked to a halt under the two big oak trees which dignified the lawn.

"I sort of maybe think," drawled Farnum, "that perhaps Mister Maxwell Vernon is in a hurry."

"Not him. Not to get anywhere, anyhow. But somebody guaranteed that car of his to do seventy miles and he's perpetually scared it's slipping. Nice kid."

"Ain't he just? Psi Tau's little ray of sunshine. Kind of undiscriminating in his choice of friends—"

"Meaning me?"

"Gosh, no. I'm talking of Mister Thayer. Anyway, I guess even a nice boy like Max is entitled to have a screw loose somewhere."

Vernon climbed from behind the wheel of his car and started toward the fraternity house. The two boys on the veranda gazed at him closely and turned inquiringly to one another.

"What's the matter with him?" inquired Gleason,

"Gee. . . . The sun is downright eclipsed, ain't it, Phil? Never did see Max looking like that. Reckon they pulled him for speeding, or something?"

There was no mistaking the fact that Max Vernon was in an ugly mood. His customarily sunny face was clouded by a scowl; he moved toward the house with short, positive

strides, his pudgy body waddling determinedly. He kept
his eyes focused on the ground and would have passed
into the house without a word of greeting had not Rube
Farnum hailed him.

"Hi! Max!"

Vernon responded without glancing at them.

"'Lo, Rube."

His manner was forbidding. Farnum, somewhat non-
plused, made a gallant attempt at cordiality.

"Pat Thayer just came in," he called cheerfully. "He's
up in his room."

Max Vernon stopped short.

"I don't give a damn where Pat Thayer is!" he growled.

As he vanished inside the house the two boys stared
in amazement. The thing was so startling that even Rube
Farnum was moved to shed his habitual lethargy. He raised
himself to a sitting posture, gazed blankly at the open
door through which Max Vernon had disappeared, and
whistled softly.

"Well, I'll be licked for a two-cent stamp! I ask you,
Phil; did you hear little Maxie?"

"Did I? Say . . . what you reckon?"

Rube shook his head in bewilderment. "I almost suspect something must have happened. Who'd ever imagine
Damon not giving a damn where Pythias was?"

"And didn't he say it like he meant it? He's sore—that
lad is. And how!"

Rube chuckled. "It only goes to prove, Philip—that
even the blindest can learn to see."

They discussed the phenomenon eagerly. Max Vernon viciously angry—and with Pat Thayer. The fraternity
house knew a great deal more about the strange intimacy
than the campus in general could ever know. They could
have told—had they cared to discuss fraternity doings—of
long sessions in Max Vernon's room on the third floor; of

a friendship so close that it was scarcely understandable—and of the meek manner in which, for the past few months at any rate, Vernon had endured innumerable snubs from Thayer.

Max's friends had long since determined that insofar as Thayer was concerned, Vernon was hopelessly blind. His display of animosity, therefore, came like a jagged lightning flash from a clear sky. Invariably, as they discussed the miracle, one or the other of them returned to the same comment.

"Mad? He acted crazy!"

"I'll say! And I never have thought Max could. I thought he was one of those chaps who was to take everything from everybody—a sort of chronic other-cheek boob."

"Something hit him hard." Rube cocked one eye at the ceiling. "You reckon it's that little blonde, Phil?"

"Larry Welch's sister?"

"Uh-huh. Max has been awful keen for her, and they do say she's been rambling around a heap with Pat lately."

"Might be. But I didn't think even a fem could jar Max like that."

"Well . . ." Rube sighed, "if I was a philosophic and observing old bird—the kind that writes textbooks—I'd make some wise comment like: You never can tell!"

They gazed off toward the street, each busy with his own thoughts. Each was happy that something had occurred between Vernon and Thayer. They detested Thayer and liked Vernon, even though they regarded him as decidedly lacking in strength of character. At least he was unaffected and friendly. Thayer was—he was—well, dog-gone it! he was Pat Thayer and they just naturally didn't like him.

Their reverie was interrupted by the arrival of a visitor. They did not notice her until she turned in on the walk and came straight toward the veranda. Then their faces broke into smiles and they jumped to their feet.

"Hey, Tony!" they hailed her. "How goes it?"

Antoinette Peyton gave each of them a brief smile.

"Hello," she said. Then her question came with startling sharpness. "Do you boys know whether Pat Thayer is in?"

It was Phil Gleason who answered.

"Yeh. He's up in his room."

"Second floor front, downhill side, isn't it, Phil?"

"Uh-huh. I'll call him for you."

And then Tony Peyton did an amazing thing: a thing so staggeringly unprecedented that neither boy was able to move a muscle.

Quite calmly Tony Peyton walked through the door and into the sacred precincts of the Psi Tau Theta fraternity house.

"Never mind," she called over her shoulder. "I'll go right up to his room."

CHAPTER IX

Tony Peyton had done the impossible—and thereby scandalized the two members of Psi Tau Theta, who stared in dumfounded amazement at the door through which she had passed. With quiet dignity and smiling determination she had calmly announced that she was going to visit the room of a fraternity member, and, what even worse—she had carried out her threat.

Had it been any other co-ed, they might have thought of stopping her. It was against all rules. Being any woman other than Tony, they would have known that the good name of the fraternity house would be forever shattered. Of course, since it was Tony—there might be criticism, but never scandal. As a matter of fact the two boys on the veranda did not know that Tony deliberately had selected this bold method of approach so that Pat Thayer would understand clearly that she was not bluffing. When a girl visits a man in his room, explanations are often necessary, and Tony—thoroughly aroused—wished the man to understand that she was prepared to let the campus know of their marriage.

The two lads presented a picture of vast amazement. Even the explosive Phil Gleason was stunned to momentary silence and Rube's jaw hung at an alarming angle. It was he, however, who first recovered the power of speech.

"Well, I'll be everlastingly dog-bit!" he murmured. "Can you beat it, Phil: I ask you."

"No!" snapped Gleason. "I can't—and neither can anybody else."

Farnum looked apprehensively up and down Fraternity Row.

"Do you reckon anybody saw her go upstairs?

"No."

"Suppose they did?"

"They couldn't, you poor simp."

"But if they did?"

"They'll tell us and we'll say they're liars. That's all. Can't let that sort of story get around the campus." Phil scratched his head. "Say, what the hell's happening around here, anyway?"

"I'll ask you."

"First Max Vernon says he don't give a damn where Pat Thayer is, and then Tony Peyton goes up to Thayer's room. I'm worried."

"So'm I, Phil. But what can we do about it?"

"Durned if I know. You reckon we ought to go up and suggest that it just ain't being done?"

"Ha-ha! Likewise—Ho-ho!—and get pitched out on our blooming necks? If there'd be one thing worse than Tony Peyton visiting Pat in his room, it would be for us to have a scrimmage with him because of it. No, sir—when two people like Pat and Tony decide to have a conversation in a place where they hadn't ought to—the best thing for a couple of young innocents like us to do is pretend we know nothing."

"Ought to be easy for you," said Gleason with a pallid flash of his caustic humor. "But for me—"

"You struggle hard," advised Rube. "Maybe you can get away with it."

They reflected heavily upon the situation, fear for the good name of their own fraternity forming their paramount worry.

"What you reckon . . ." started Farnum and Gleason answered the unfinished question.

"Nothing, except that Tony is straight as they make 'em. If they were pulling any rough stuff you can bet your last dollar they wouldn't do it in the open that way. It's O.K., Rube—but dog-gone indiscreet."

For twenty minutes Rube Farnum and Phil Gleason sat on the veranda in miserable uncertainty. There was absolutely nothing they could do to rectify an impossible situation, and they were doing it with all the ill grace in the world.

But at twenty minutes past one Tony appeared on the veranda again. They glanced at her and saw that she seemed to be laboring under stress of some powerful emotion. They also noticed that she was making a brave effort to appear casual. Awkwardly, the two boys rose and bowed. They uttered somewhat fatuous remarks.

Tony gave them a hard little smile and said good-by. She walked to the street and turned uphill toward Old Main. Rube sank back into his hammock with a sigh of infinite relief.

"And that," he remarked—"is most decidedly that."

"Yeh. But what is it?"

"Durned if I know. Say, Phil—did you get a good flash at her?"

"I didn't get anything else."

"What did those dead orbs of yours notice?"

"Hmm. . . . You tell me."

"She seemed kind of worked up. Right mad, I might say."

"She did. Sore as a goat. What you reckon?"

"There's something funny. . . . And I think the more we say nothing the less we'll get mixed up in a scandal. First of all I thought Tony was just dumb going up to his room. Now I don't think so. She knew she'd thrown a fast one, and was trying to make us think she didn't know it—or something of the sort."

A slender young person with clothes of howlingly collegiate pattern, descended from the veranda of the Rho Tau Sigma house and ambled across the street. Gleason grabbed his friend's arm.

"Here comes little poison ivy," he said grimly. "All we know is nothing, and we ain't sure of that."

"I gotcha!"

The newcomer joined Farnum and Gleason. He draped himself languidly over the veranda railing.

"Wasn't that Tony Peyton that came out of your house just now?" he inquired lazily.

Rube turned upon him an expression of utter guilelessness.

"Sure," he answered. "Sure it was."

"Thought so." The visitor lighted a cigarette with elaborate nonchalance. "Looked like she came down from upstairs."

Phil Gleason laughed merrily. "Give ear to Sherlock Holmes. You haven't seen any pink bananas flitting from tree to tree, have you?"

"No-o, but it seemed like—"

Rube Farnum spoke quietly; but there was something in his voice which gave warning to the visitor from across the street.

"I don't exactly figure what you're driving at," said Rube with chill friendliness; "but it don't sound awful good to a Psi Tau—of which I am one of whom. Tony Peyton came here to see Pat Thayer. They were in the reception room yonder."

"You could see 'em?"

"Certainly. From right where we were sitting. And it don't hardly make any enormous hit with me for you to make remarks like you have been doing."

"I see . . . I didn't mean anything."

"I'm downright glad you didn't, Nelson. I sure am. We're right jealous of our own respectability over here, and we don't relish criticism from the other side of the Row."

"I wasn't criticizing. Honest, I wasn't."

"Sure not. And one more thing before you go: any one else should happen to ask me if Tony Peyton went upstairs in this fraternity house, I'd naturally start wondering where he ever got such an idea. And maybe I might think the suggestion came from Mister Howard Nelson. Of course, I know you wouldn't do anything so ungentlemanly as to talk about something which you thought you saw—'specially when you know you're mistaken . . . but I was just expressing the hope, for the sake of everybody's good health, that nobody else would ask me that question. You savvy, Mister Nelson?"

Mister Nelson stared at Rube Farnum. Rube's good-natured face was queerly stern and Mister Nelson was not inclined to argue. He beat a rather hasty, and not entirely dignified, retreat. Rube stared after him.

"If that pup lets out one single crack—"

"He won't," chuckled Gleason. "You scared him plumb to death."

Rube glanced at his watch. "Did you say you had a one-twenty class, Phil?"

"Had is right. I've cut it."

"I'll say you have. It's one-forty-five now. You don't care how bad a scholastic record you compile, do you?"

"Well, no . . . now that you mention it. I—"

There was a sound of feet on the stairway inside the fraternity house. The boys looked toward the door in time to see Max Vernon come out.

His manner still puzzled them. The moonlike face was sternly set, giving it a somewhat grotesque appearance of futile anger; he was moving with short, quick strides across the veranda.

He was wearing a different suit from the one which had adorned his figure a half hour since and he seemed even more engrossed with thoughts of no highly pleasant nature.

He descended to the walk without so much as a glance at Farnum and Gleason. They noticed that under his arm he carried a sizable bundle. They saw him reach his car and pitch the bundle into the tonneau. Then, with more speed than grace, Vernon jumped behind the wheel, kicked the starter, clashed his gears savagely and jerked into the road. They saw him start downhill at reckless speed and once again they looked at each other inquiringly.

"Something's puzzling me," remarked Rube slowly.

"What?"

"Which is the most remarkable phenomenon: Tony Peyton's visit to Pat Thayer's room, or Max Vernon's wild-eyed fury. I ask you, Phil—which?"

Gleason gave a prompt and explicit answer.

"Both!" he said tersely.

CHAPTER X

Ivy Welch emerged from the woman's dormitory and confronted her brother. Her dress of pale blue revealed quite frankly the immaturity of her figure and Larry, gazing down at her with big-brotherly affection, found it difficult to reconcile himself to the idea that any affair of the heart in which Ivy was concerned was to be taken seriously. But her first words sounded the alarm. She met his eyes levelly and spoke without equivocation.

"I know exactly why you've come, Larry. It's to tell me I've got to quit Pat Thayer. The answer is that I won't do it."

The tolerant smile died on his lips, and he frowned slightly.

"Why, Ivy?"

"Because I love him."

He shook his head. "You're seventeen years old."

"Lots of girls have been married at seventeen. And I guess I'm old enough to know my own mind."

"Not about a man like Thayer, Sis."

She stamped her tiny foot. "Tony Peyton has been talking to you, hasn't she? She's been filling you full of poison. She's just jealous, that's all."

"No-o," he answered soberly, "she's not jealous."

"How do you know?"

"I know it."

"Hmph!" Ivy spoke with the superiority of womanly intuition. "I guess she's got the wool pulled over your eyes, too. I guess I could see that she was jealous when she caught us in the Bower. I mean I could tell by every single word she said."

"She isn't jealous, Ivy. I feel confident of that."

"Yes; because you're crazy about her—that's why. You take my advice, Bud, and lay off her. She's playing you off against Pat."

He smiled. "You see," he explained, "I didn't come over to ask advice. I came to give it."

"I appreciate it, Bud. But I guess I understand this better than you do."

"No. You've got to quit Thayer."

"I've *got* to?"

"Yes."

Her lips pressed tightly together. "Since when did you start telling me what I must do?"

"It's for your own good."

"Oh, yes—because a jealous woman wants the man who's crazy about me: that's why. And because she's got you fooled. Honest, I never would have thought Tony Peyton could be so small and mean."

"She isn't that, Sis; believe me, I know what I'm talking about. She told me a good deal—"

"—About this afternoon?"

"About other things."

"What?"

He hesitated. "I'm not at liberty to say."

"No. Certainly you aren't. I'm ashamed of you, Bud. You're not playing fair. I guess if it's so important that I keep away from Pat Thayer it's important enough for you to tell me what you know."

"I promised Tony—"

"Naturally, she'd make you promise; because most likely whatever she said isn't so."

"That isn't very nice, Sis."

"And is it nice for you to come knocking Pat Thayer when you know I'm crazy about him? Is it?"

He tried to be fair. "I guess it sounds pretty bad," he confessed. "But you know I'm honest, Sis—and what I'm telling you isn't guesswork. It isn't based on rumor. Thayer isn't any man for you."

"Who's the best judge?"

"I am," he repeated patiently. "And I don't want you going with him any more."

Ivy frowned angrily. "I don't care what you want."

"You must lay off him."

"There you go again. I don't *have* to do what you say. I guess if you weren't at this college I'd do what I want, and you promised never to horn in—"

"But when you need protection, Sis—"

"I'll be obliged if you'll butt right out, too. And I'm not going to fool you, Bud. I'll be with Pat as much as he wants me to, and I guess that'll be a good little bit."

"Even if I ask you not to?"

"Even then. Now listen—" She stepped close and put her hand on his sleeve. "I know you mean well, Bud, but you're all wet on this. Pat is a swell fellow. And he's crazy about me—"

"Not that bird!"

"Stop!" Unconsciously, she became quite melodramatic. "I'm not going to let even you talk about Pat that way."

"No-o? I guess if I know he's rotten . . ."

"Oh! That isn't fair, Larry. It isn't. You're being nasty about Pat and you don't know anything. Well, I guess he's told me all the bad things about himself that any one else knows, and I love him. I'm going to keep on going with him, and I won't have you interfering."

Her slim figure grew tense. And Larry, gazing down at her in bewilderment, was beginning to discover that he did not know his little sister as well as he had thought. She seemed queerly womanly for all her extreme youth, and certainly there was no misunderstanding her intentions.

"I shall positively stick with Pat. Now—are you going to leave us alone?"

"No," he said honestly, "I'm not."

"I warn you, Bud—you'd better."

His eyes narrowed. "What do you mean: I'd better?"

"I mean this," she said slowly. "If you try to keep Pat Thayer and me apart, I'll marry him!"

"You'll *what?*"

"I'll marry him."

"Don't be silly—"

"I'm not silly, and you'll find it out mighty quick. I'm crazy about Pat . . . but if you won't leave us alone I'll marry him the first chance I get."

"But—but you can't!"

"Because you say so?"

He cursed himself. He wished he hadn't told Tony that he'd keep her secret.

"You—you just can't, that's all," he said lamely.

"We'll see." She was aflame with indignation: "I'm going to ask him myself if he'll marry me! And don't think I don't mean that, Bud—because I do!"

He stared at her for a minute. She was his sister—and he knew that she was serious. He was bewildered. Until the last few moments she had always rather amused him. It had never occurred to him that she wasn't still a mere child.

"You're a little fool!" he snapped tactlessly.

She tossed her head.

"Hmph!" she commented and the sniff was more expressive than many words.

He sensed the futility of further argument and turned away abruptly. She jumped in front of him, her eyes blazing.

"Where are you going, Larry?"

His face was more grim and forbidding than she had ever seen it.

"I can't hammer any sense into your head, Ivy—so I'm going to see Pat Thayer."

"Oh . . . you wouldn't dare!"

"No?"

"You'll be starting something!" She was trembling violently and her face was pale with anger. "I warn you, Larry— you'll be starting something."

He moved away. "You're darn right I will," he said sharply.

She stood like a little statue as he strode off down the path which led through the glen and so up the hill opposite; the hill on which the college buildings were clustered. Then she whirled and vanished into the dormitory, where she sought the sanctuary of her own room for a hysterical cry.

And he, striding moodily past the vine-screened entrance of the Bower, knew that he was dealing with a desperate situation.

He tried to think clearly; tried to rid himself of the prejudice which must necessarily arise because Tony Peyton was the other woman in the case. Of course, he didn't believe that Thayer would commit bigamy . . . but there were so many things an egotistical and unscrupulous man might do when a young and pretty girl threw herself at his head.

One thing was very clear to Larry Welch in that moment of worry; he must see Thayer immediately. There must be a show-down. He couldn't handle but his teeth clenched as he reflected upon the fact that he could mighty well handle Pat Thayer.

It was a pity that he couldn't tell Thayer that Tony had explained everything. That would simplify things. As it was, he had to approach the man and warn him to remain away from Ivy. Perhaps the scene would not be very tranquil. Thayer himself was a big man and a powerful one, despite his dissipations. And none of the ugly rumors circulating about the campus had ever imputed cowardice.

Actually, Larry experienced an exultation at the prospect that Thayer might not be easy to handle. Ivy had roused him more than he knew. He was boiling internally, and he wanted a vent for his overwrought feelings. He mounted the hill with determined strides; moved swiftly across the campus, circled the Main Building and descended Fraternity Row.

Rube Farnum and Phil Gleason were still lounging on the veranda of the Psi Tau Theta house. It was Rube who saw Larry first.

"And now another," he drawled. "Here comes Larry Welch looking like some one had socked him below the belt. If precedent means anything he's coming straight here."

But even Farnum did not take his own words seriously, and so his jaw dropped as Larry passed his own fraternity house and turned in at Psi Tau Theta. And as though that were not enough to complete the consternation of the two boys, his single question as he crossed the veranda completely flattened them.

"Pat Thayer in?" he asked.

"Yeh . . . upstairs."

Then, when he had entered the house, they looked at one another bewilderedly.

"My brain has just plumb stopped functioning," breathed Rube.

"You flatter yourself!" snapped Gleason. "But I can join you in asking what th' 'ell?"

The affair was too puzzling for mere conversation. Occasionally one would shake his head, but speech was not necessary. Each knew that the other was thinking in circles.

"I'll say this much," commented Gleason after a five-minute silence: "Pat Thayer has sure gotten popular with a mixed crowd."

"Yeh . . ." agreed Rube. "Or unpopular!"

For five minutes more nothing happened. Then, at ten minutes past two o'clock, Larry Welch appeared in the doorway.

He did not pause. He crossed the veranda with quick steps and descended to the walk in a single jump. The two boys stared after him, then directed their gazes toward each other.

"Happy lad," commented Gleason. "He looked almost scared."

"Ain't it the truth? You reckon—"

"I don't reckon anything. All I know is I'd hate to have Larry Welch get as sore at me as he seems to be at somebody right now. I never knew that bird could get real angry."

"No-o . . . and we didn't either of us know that Max Vernon could be all riled up. Or that Tony Peyton would visit a man in our fraternity house. Seems like to me, Phil, we're in the throes of living and learning."

"Learning what?"

"Something we'll never understand—like higher math."

That was the one point upon which the two young men agreed. It was downright spooky how the three occurrences of the past ninety minutes had impressed them. They felt vaguely uncomfortable . . . nervous even. Rube smoked several cigarettes in rapid succession and finally Gleason extended his hand for one.

"You smoking?" was Farnum's amazed comment.

"Yes—you idiot! I'm jumpy!"

He puffed deeply on the cigarette, hoping that it would soothe his nerves.

At fifteen minutes after two o'clock . . . almost before the mellow chimes of the quarter hour had died out from the tower of Old Main . . . something happened: something eerily terrible, something which jarred the two students to their feet and caused cold sweat to break out on their foreheads.

From upstairs in the fraternity house there came a wild shriek; an inhuman howl. There was an instant's pause and then the howl was repeated and there was a sound of feet running heavily down the stairway, and on the summer air certain words came to the startled ears of the two boys.

"Oh! God . . . oh, my God! . . ."

Quivering with a fright they could not entirely understand, they moved toward the front door. But before they reached it a human figure catapulted onto the veranda; a disheveled, wild-eyed figure which was making passionate gestures and struggling futilely to say something.

They recognized him instantly: Mike Carmicino, janitor of the fraternity house. He grabbed Farnum's arm. He tried to talk, but no words came; only the gibberish of terror.

And finally Farnum shook himself loose. He grabbed Carmicino by the shoulder and glared at him.

"What's the matter?" he asked hoarsely. "Wh-what's all the yelling about?"

Carmicino gestured wildly toward the interior of the house.

"Meester Thayer!" he croaked—"Meester Thayer!"

"What about him?"

Carmicino covered his eyes with his hands.

"He is dead!" he groaned. "Somebody have murdered Meester Thayer!"

CHAPTER XI

Over the bowed head of the babbling, crouching, shaken, sobbing janitor, the two fraternity brothers faced each other. Their eyes were distended with horror as they struggled to comprehend the message which Mike Carmicino brought to them. They did not speak immediately, but their thoughts were identical: a frantic review of the succession of unconventional and unusual happenings; a leaping from one conclusion to another, and—naturally enough—a depressing fear that the events of the past hour would hopelessly besmirch the good name of Psi Tau Theta.

Phil Gleason took one of Carmicino's arms and Rube Farnum the other. They led the janitor to a chair, where he bent forward, his squat, muscular body racked with dry sobs. The boys were badly shaken, but at least they tried to think clearly, and Farnum's voice, when he questioned the janitor, was almost steady.

"You say Mr. Thayer is dead?"

Carmicino shuddered.

"*Si-si,* Signore. He is quite completely murdered."

"You are sure?"

The janitor raised his wild, black eyes to their faces.

"Of course, I am sure. He is on the floor of hees room. There is much blood. He does not breathe. Hees heart it does not beat. I am quite sure he is dead."

"Good Lord. . . . How did you find him?"

"I go upstairs to the room of Meester MacLeod. I see the door of Meester Thayer's room is not entirely shut. I look in and I see one foot and one leg on the floor. I theenk that is very funny that Meester Thayer should lie on the floor and not move. Perhaps he is drunk, I think, because it is a pretty day and sometimes often Meester Thayer say that is excuse for getting drunk. So I think I will put him on the bed and shut the door so nobody will know he is drunk. I go in the room and then I see the blood—and—and—"

"And what?"

"I stand there for a minute. Two minutes. I do not understand that Meester Thayer what is so kind to me have come to a sad ending. Then I see he is dead and something grab me right here—" He touched his throat with a dramatic gesture. "I cannot breathe. I cannot move. I am scared."

"You—you mean some one really grabbed you?"

"No!" Mike's eyes rolled with terror at the very thought. "I mean I feel as bad like somebody does that. I am scared. I am frighten'. I try to move and I cannot make no success of moving. And so I yell. I yell very loud—"

"God! I'll say you did."

"—And then I run downstairs."

"You—you didn't touch the body?"

"Only so much that I could tell he was dead."

Gleason looked up. "We'd better 'phone the police, Rube."

"Gosh. . . . Think of what this means to the fraternity."

"That's none of our business. If we don't call the cops we'll get ourselves mixed up in this. And I guess we'd better 'phone the Dean, too."

Gleason walked unsteadily into the fraternity house and called the Marland police station. Then he telephoned to the Dean and returned to the porch. He seated himself in the hammock beside the stricken figure of Rube Farnum.

It was a ghastly thing—made even more grisly by the perfect day; the sensuous, flower-scented breezes of first summer; the carefree, strolling groups of students; the atmosphere of perfect peace and contentment which pervaded Fraternity and the campus beyond Old Main. Spring flowers blooming in profusion; trees garlanded with the brilliant green of early summer; preparations for the class track and field meet in the afternoon; portent of the year's end . . . laughter and jollity and careless youth. And upstairs the body of a young man lying dead. Murdered. It wasn't believable. The two young men were appalled by their own knowledge of surrounding circumstances. There was so much they knew which might prove damning. They visioned themselves being grilled in court . . . perhaps being arrested as material witnesses. They were completely and thoroughly frightened.

A small car whirled into the Row from Marland Road and chugged up the hill. It jerked to a halt in front of the fraternity house and two men alighted. One of them was tall and broad and wore the uniform of the Marland police force. The other, wearing civilian clothes, was short and squat, although he moved with the quick, certain tread of the well-conditioned, powerful athlete.

Students strolling on the Row or lounging on the verandas of fraternity houses, stared with sudden interest at Psi Tau Theta. There was a general movement in the direction of the house. Wild rumor flew from lip to lip. A liquor raid! Didn't those fool police have any judgment? A young man from Lambda Beta Pi addressed the uniformed policeman who stood on the lawn of Psi Tau Theta.

"What's wrong, officer?"

The cop answered tersely.

"Murder!"

"Good God. . . . You don't mean . . ."

"I don't mean nothin', young feller. Somebody's been murdered in yonder and nobody's to go in or git out. That's all."

The startled young man told his companion. The news sped from lip to lip. It flashed across the campus like a noxious wave. There was a period of stunned, shocked silence followed by a flood of fierce conjecture and unfounded rumor. Murder in the Psi Tau Theta house! It wasn't so! It couldn't be! Things like that just didn't happen in quiet little universities like Marland.

Who was it? No, not Rube Farnum: he had been seen on the porch. Then somebody mentioned Pat Thayer. Many persons mentioned Pat Thayer. No one knew where the rumor started, but Thayer's name was on every lip. The policeman on the lawn either didn't know or wouldn't say, and he allowed nobody to approach within hearing distance of the group on the veranda: the militant, positive figure of John Reagan, chief of the Marland plainclothes force; a pleasant enough man who was unquestionably efficient; Mike Carmicino, the janitor, petrified with fear and trembling violently—occasionally talking torrentially and at other times appalled to silence; Rube Farnum, tall and limp and frightened; Phil Gleason, reduced from his customary alertness to a shriveled miniature of his usual positive self.

That was all the students could see. They knew nothing, although somehow the rumor persisted that Pat Thayer was the man who had been killed. The crowds which poured down from the campus and thronged the lawn in front of the fraternity house asked a million questions and received a million different answers. All any one knew was what some one else had said—and ideas and theories emerged from nowhere and took shape as they passed from tongue to tongue.

Reagan was questioning Farnum. He was doing it kindly but keenly. Rube was struggling to be fair and honest: to remember things and yet to avoid injustice to any one. He wished himself well out of it. Even in the calcium glare, he was absolutely and abysmally miserable.

Then there emerged from the Main Building a tall and dignified man before whom a path opened in the throng of students. Whitman Boyd, Dean of Marland, turned in before the tragic fraternity house and was promptly stopped by the policeman on duty.

"No further for you," snapped the officer, and then, in deference to the Dean's obvious dignity, appended a "Sir."

Dean Boyd spoke quietly, in a rich, musical voice.

"Are you in charge, Officer?"

"Out here I am."

"I mean, on this case?"

"No. That'll be John Reagan yonder." And he gestured toward the veranda.

"Will you ask him if I may speak to him? I'm Dean of this college and I'd like to find out what has happened."

The policeman called out to Reagan. "This guy is the big boss, Chief. Can he come up?"

Reagan's keen eyes surveyed the Dean. He jerked his head affirmatively.

"Let him through."

The Dean mounted the veranda steps, his arrival sending a glow of thanksgiving through the breasts of Rube Farnum and Phil Gleason. He spoke directly to Reagan.

"My name is Whitman Boyd," he said quietly. "I don't know what has happened and I'd like to find out."

"So would I, Mr. Boyd. It's trouble enough."

"I understand that some one has been killed."

"Murdered. Young feller named Thayer."

"Good God! Then it's true—"

"What do you mean," snapped Reagan: "It's true?"

"I mean I heard the students gossiping. They said they thought it was Thayer."

"You've heard nothing else?"

"No. That's why I came. To find out."

"Well—he's dead all right enough. Stabbed in the throat. 'Taint pleasant up in that room." He motioned toward Farnum and Gleason. "What do you know about these two birds?"

"They are very fine boys." Both men could hear the two fine boys sigh with relief.

"And I'll tell you," interrupted Gleason earnestly, "that we haven't left the porch. Howard Nelson has been watching us from the Rho Tau Sigma house and he knows we haven't left this veranda. We can prove that."

"I didn't ask you to prove nothing, did I? Not yet."

The Dean shook his head.

"What do you wish done, Mr. Reagan?"

"Just exactly nothing," said the detective crisply. "Right now I'm gonna 'phone headquarters for a couple more harness bulls to police the grounds. Nobody's to come in here and no one's to leave. These three fellers ain't to move from where they are."

"You mean," gasped Gleason, "that we're under arrest?"

John Reagan grinned broadly. "Not yet you ain't, young feller. But don't get impatient."

CHAPTER XII

The town of Marland spreads fanwise from the foot of the hill on which stand the buildings of the University. Originally, it was a collection of sparsely traveled roads which debouched in all directions from the college. In later years a few residents of the city, some twenty miles away, decide that they desired the fresh air of the country and so the first estates were established in Marland.

Since then the community has grown into a town of some fifteen thousand persons. Limited commercially and industrially by its proximity to a big city, it has developed handsome homes and homes that are merely pretty. It covers a huge area; an area out of all proportion to its size or civic importance—a fact of which its citizens are very proud. It boasts two country clubs and a neat, busy little shopping center where housewives do their marketing; and where flourish small specialty shops for busy buyers who have neither time nor inclination for the twenty-mile journey into the city.

Oak Street, some three miles from the University, is the chief shopping center of Marland. Southward from its intersection with sparsely settled Archer Street, one finds three blocks of neat stores: groceries, butcher shops, cafeterias, drug stores with gleaming soda fountains—and two

motion picture theaters. But despite Oak Street's importance as a shopping thoroughfare, it is not a main traffic
artery? which is, perhaps, a tactical advantage.

Archer Street carries the traffic load. It runs east and
west. At the former terminus is the city. Its western end
is indeterminate . . . it merely vanishes into the country
somewhere, and spreads out into a series of unpaved roads
which bear a University reputation as being good spots for
parking.

At the four corners which mark the intersection of Oak
and Archer there are two gas filling stations and two drug
stores. The latter, however, open on Oak Street, and next
to one of them, one door from the corner, facing Archer
Street and west of Oak, is the snug little gray stone home
of the Marland National Bank.

The Marland National bears an enviable reputation. It
is small but staunch, and on its roster of directors one will
find names which carry great weight even in the city of
a quarter million which exists twenty miles away. To the
left of the Marland National there is a vacant lot which
the bank owns—and holds for a proper price. Beyond that
lot there are a few residences of an exceedingly modest
type, for it is not considered very swank to live on Archer
Street. Across the way is one of the gas filling stations and
next to that place a lumber and coal yard.

But despite its aloofness, the granite building presents
a front of great dignity. It is spoken of boastfully by natives
of Marland, and Randolph Fiske, its president, is a real
power in the community.

This morning—the morning of May third—Randolph
Fiske sat at his desk in the office which was marked "President—Private." He was a tall, well-proportioned man, fifty-
eight years of age, whose hair matched the gray of his
bank building. He had a fine, broad forehead and iron-
gray brows from beneath which a pair of keen black eyes

peered in a manner which gave an impression of unim-
peachable efficiency.

And Randolph Fiske was efficient, as witness the
glass-covered top of his great walnut desk. Two or three
papers, an unopened letter . . . and nothing else. One
never found Fiske's office cluttered with unfinished work,
nor piled high with confusing documents. He attended
to one thing at a time; completed his task—and banished
all traces of it to the various safes and files. Now he was
gazing attentively at a tiny bit of pasteboard which had
been placed in his hand by an angular and hawklike lady
of very uncertain years.

It was plain that Mr. Fiske was more than a trifle interested in the card, despite the fact that it was not immaculately clean. There was printing on its surface—printing,
not embossing. It said simply:

JAMES H. HANVEY
BANKERS' PROTECTIVE ASS'N.

Mr. Fiske eye roved to a yellow telegram which had
arrived two days previously from New York. It was from
headquarters of the Bankers' Protective Association and
was very explicit.

OUR BEST OPERATIVE ARRIVES MAR-
LAND MORNING MAY THIRD.

This, then, was the man. Mr. Fiske heaved a sigh of
relief as he prepared to shift a very great burden to the
shoulders of another man—one professionally equipped to
bear such burdens. He looked up at Miss Seward.

"Show Mr. Hanvey in, please."

Miss Seward put out a bony hand which trembled in
protest.

"Surely, Mr. Fiske—not *that* man!"

"Not which man?"

"The—the terrible person who gave me that card."

Fiske frowned.

"I don't understand, Miss Seward. This man is a great detective."

A thin and superior smile played about the corners of Miss Seward's lips.

"There's a mistake, Mr. Fiske. This person couldn't detect anything. I'm very sure of that."

"What makes you think so?" There was a hint of ice in Mr. Fiske's voice, but for once it did not frighten Miss Seward.

"Oh, lots!" she answered. "Just wait until you see him."

She vanished in triumph, and Randolph Fiske stared after her. "What in the world. . . ?" Then he smiled. At least she had prepared him for a somewhat uncouth person. Probably a squat gentleman with a brown derby, square-toed shoes, a checkered vest and a dime's worth of chewing tobacco. Queer how these detective chaps always dressed so that there was no mistaking their profession. Randolph Fiske saw the door swing open. He caught a flash of Miss Seward's hatchet face with its triumphant smirk which seemed to say loudly: "I told you so." Then the door closed and Mr. Fiske was rendered inarticulate.

He found himself gazing upon a grotesque, Brobding-nagian figure about which a cheap and shiny suit of blue serge hung with alarming looseness. Was it possible? Fiske drew a deep breath . . . he glanced again at the card, then resumed his amazed survey of the visitor.

Jim Hanvey was massive rather than picturesque. He was everything in the world which one is quite sure a detective should not be. His two hundred and sixty pounds of avoirdupois was distributed with heavily inartistic effect; it wabbled when he moved . . . and he seemed to move with vast reluctance.

But it was the head which rose above triple chins that filled Randolph Fiske with awe. The chins afforded a cushion for the big head—like shock absorbers beneath a truck. The face was huge and round and utterly expressionless. Randolph Fiske was quite sure that never before in his life had he seen a human countenance so utterly devoid of intelligence. It was—yes, by George!—it was the eyes! Round little eyes which were as vacant and colorless as the orbs of a fish. And even while Fiske stared, Hanvey's lids dropped with maddening slowness over those eyes; held shut just long enough for Mr. Fiske to become convinced that the detective had gone to sleep . . . and then uncurtained with the same deliberateness.

The mass of flesh stood in the doorway. He was impressive—as a mountain is impressive. Fiske knew he was breathing; he could tell that by the fact that a rather remarkable contraption which appeared in the neighborhood of Jim Hanvey's prodigious tummy kept moving rhythmically. Randolph Fiske kept his eyes fascinatedly on that particular apparatus. It held him spellbound. It hung from a hawserlike watch chain and was similar to nothing which the banker had ever before set eyes upon. It was long and slim and seemed to be made of gold.

Then, without warning, the silence was punctured by a sleep, drawly voice.

"It's a toothpick, Mr. Fiske."

"Huh?" The banker jerked himself together. He could hardly believe that the sound had emerged from the lips of the fleshy giant. "Wh-what's a toothpick?"

"This." Hanvey touched the trinket affectionately and detached it from his chain. "Swellest piece of joolry I've got. A crook friend gave it to me. It's solid gold—eighteen karat. Great invention: feller don't always have to be running around hunting toothpicks when he's got one of these. Look!" He touched a spring and a wicked little blade leaped out at Randolph Fiske. That gentleman gave a perceptible jump.

"It—it's very—very remarkable," he murmured.

Hanvey reattached the toothpick to the chain. It seemed to be an important and tedious job. The banker was trying to adjust himself. He was staring and wondering . . . and then the opaque eyes of Jim Hanvey were raised slowly until they met the gaze of the banker. Hanvey spoke.

"I *am* kind of funny-looking, ain't I, Mr. Fiske?"

CHAPTER XIII

Mr. Randolph Fiske was completely stripped of the poise upon which he prided himself. In appearance, wardrobe and manner his visitor was quite an amazing person. And so Mr. Fiske did not answer and Hanvey made another remark.

"Feller can't help bein' fat, can he? That is, not unless he's willing to quit eating and roll around on the floor every morning and do a lot of other dam' fool things."

Mr. Fiske shook his head and murmured a polite "I guess not."

"Sure not. I reckon I was born fat—and lazy. Folks always look at me like you're doing when they first see me, so don't you be embarrassed. I've got a skin thicker than a pair of rhinoceroses."

Fiske picked up the slightly soiled card which lay on his desk.

"You are James H. Hanvey?"

"Uh-huh. In person. Largely, I may say."

"You're a *detective?*"

"Well—that's putting it kind of strong, Mr. Fiske. It all depends on what you call a detective."

"I mean—you are the man the B. P. A. sent down here to investigate the robbery?"

"Yeh."

Mr. Fiske was getting himself under control. He sought refuge in frankness.

"I imagine my actions have been exceedingly discourteous, Mr. Hanvey. I apologize and only wish to explain that you somewhat startled me. You see, my idea of a detective has been formed from the reading of fiction and you are not—well, not exactly the sort of detective about which I've read."

"I wish I was," breathed Hanvey ecstatically. Gosh! I love mystery stories. Them fellers sure are slick. I never could figure out how they do their tricks."

Another shock for the banker. He blinked.

"And you don't work like the detectives in books?"

"Golly, no. I ain't slick, Mr. Fiske. I don't hardly know any dicks who are."

"Then how—?"

"Lemme tell you something." Hanvey leaned confidentially across the desk and his sleepy eyes held the attention of the banker. "My kind of work ain't so hard. And why? Suppose I go on a case. I start off wrong. All right, nobody's the wiser, and when I find out I'm on the wrong track—I start again. Same thing always. A detective can make all the mistakes in the world, Mr. Fiske—but if he happens to do one thing right—he lands the man he's after: see?"

"Yes—I see."

"But the crook, gosh! the poor feller hasn't got a chance. If he slips just one time, he's caught. He has to do everything right. The detective only has to do one thing right. And there you are. It ain't no mystery—except how a crook ever gets away."

"Then there's nothing to all this theory of deduction?"

"We-e-ell, maybe so, Mr. Fiske. I ain't educated and don't know much about theories and things. But I ain't hardly ever seen a dick that deducted any thing much—unless it was expense money."

Fiske had been studying his visitor. He amazed now to find himself warming to the ungainly person. There was an almost childish simplicity about Hanvey which gave Fiske confidence—although he told himself that the man was a caricature.

"The B. P. A. wired me," he said slowly, "that you are their best operative."

"Hooey!" grinned Hanvey. "I've just been lucky—that's all."

"A man can't always be lucky."

"I can. You see, it's this way: Most all the crooks are my friends, and they don't lie to me—so that makes things pretty easy."

The banker gasped. "Crooks are your friends?"

"Sure. Why not?"

"I—I never heard of such a thing."

"I guess not. But can't you see how much easier it makes things?"

"You say they don't lie to you?"

"Well, the high-class crooks don't. Only the bums."

"Good Lord!" Fiske leaned back in his chair and regarded Hanvey with wide-eyed wonder. "You are quite the most remarkable man I've ever met."

"And the fattest?"

For the first time, Fiske smiled.

"And the fattest."

Hanvey's eyes twinkled for a moment. He fumbled in the breast pocket of his coat and produced two thin and vicious-looking projectiles. He extended these toward his companion.

"Have a cigar?"

Fiske thanked him and accepted one. Hanvey bit the end from the other, held a match to it and inhaled with

vast relish. He blew a cloud of smoke across the room and
Fiske turned startled eyes in his direction.

"They *are* kind of strong," said the detective genially.
"Some folks don't like 'em."

Fiske struggled heroically against the asphyxiating effect of the violent fumes. Then they got the better of him.

"May—may I open another window?" he inquired weakly.

"Sure. That'll be fine." Hanvey eyed the second cigar
which lay unlighted on the desk. "Ain't you going to smoke
yours?"

"I'll try one of my own if you don't mind."

As the banker moved toward the window, Jim sighed
relievedly. He rescued the unused cigar and tucked it back
in his breast pocket with real affection. Jim's cigars were a
source of perpetual worry: he was always afraid that some
day some one would smoke one of them.

Fiske seated himself again and stared at his visitor.
Hanvey seemed to be asleep. Quite obviously he had no
intention of mentioning the matter which had brought
him to Marland.

Fiske was beginning to like the man. He was an astounding person, but somehow one could not resist him. He
had an uncanny way of knowing what one was thinking.
Fiske hesitated, but only for a moment.

"You'd like to hear about the robbery?" he asked suddenly.

"Yeh—if you want."

"Isn't that what you came for?"

"Reckon so."

"Then why don't you ask me some questions?"

"Gosh! Mr. Fiske—how do I know what to ask? I'm
waiting for you to tell me, and you're waiting until you're
sure I didn't escape from some zoo."

Randolph Fiske threw back his head and laughed. "You
win, Hanvey. Now—shoot!"

Jim's face did not change expression. He spoke in the same quiet monotone.

"When?"

"Day before yesterday—May first—at ten minutes after two o'clock."

"How much?"

"The robber got away with approximately one hundred thousand dollars in currency."

Hanvey blinked. "Lot of cash for a little bank like this."

"Plenty. We were making up the pay roll for the Marland Mills. They pay on the third."

"Stick-up?" queried the detective.

"Yes."

"Tell me all about it."

Fiske rose and invited Hanvey to follow him. They passed from his private office into the bank proper. It was a long room with marble floor and counters and was lined on both sides with bronze, barred cages. Under the amazed eyes of Miss Helen Seward, Fiske conducted Hanvey to the front door and gestured to the broad thoroughfare passing east and west.

"That is Archer Street," said Fiske. "The north and south street is Oak. Oak is a shopping street, but Archer is the main traffic artery. Lots of cars going by here all the time." He designated a device which hung in the middle of the street intersection. "We even have a traffic light, you see. You will also notice that this bank is the only commercial establishment on Archer Street. Even the drug store next to us faces on Oak. Do you follow me?"

"Easy," grunted Jim. "You sure do talk explicit."

Fiske stepped back into the bank. "This double door here is glass, you notice. We have two plate glass windows, one on each side of the door. Our banking business starts at nine in the morning and stops at two. At two o'clock daily—and on Saturdays at twelve—we get rid of our last customer. Then we conceal the interior of the bank by pulling the shades—so."

He stepped behind the open door and pulled a shade which rose up from the bottom of the door. The heavy green shade rose along the glass surface until it was higher than a man's head.

"There are similar curtains on both windows," he went on. "By a few minutes after two o'clock every day—when these curtains are raised from the bottom—no one can see into the bank from outside, but our clerks have plenty of light to work by because the daylight comes in through the upper half. You understand?"

"Sure."

"Good. As soon as we get the last customer out, we pull the curtains up, and then all of the employees except two or three go out for a bite of lunch. They invariably go out the back door. That door, which is behind my office, opens onto a little alley through which you can pass into Oak Street. All the lunch rooms are on Oak and we always go in and out that way. Day before yesterday the bank was free of customers at two o'clock. We drew the curtains and shut the front doors."

"Were they locked?"

"No. They never are. We have safety vaults in the basement and they are open until five o'clock. There has to be some way for clients to get into the building. We merely shut the doors and draw the curtains to keep our banking clients out. Those who rent boxes here know that they can get in at any time."

Fiske turned away, but Hanvey examined the door. He saw that it was equipped on the inside with a heavy spring lock. He turned and followed the banker, apparently unconscious of the startled and amused glances which followed his huge, waddling figure.

Back in Fiske's office, the banker resumed his story. Hanvey lolled in a chair, apparently asleep. But occasionally his eyes uncurtained for a moment and he regarded the banker gravely before closing them again.

"May first was a perfect day," said Fiske. "We'd had a chilly and rainy April, but with the coming of May the weather turned perfect. Warm and sunshiny and almost like summer."

Hanvey mopped at a perspiring forehead. "It's entirely like summer now," he wheezed.

"As I said, we shut the door and drew the curtain at two o'clock sharp, so that the interior of the bank was effectually concealed from any one on the street. At the same time everybody went out to lunch except Miss Seward and myself."

"Miss Seward?"

"She is my secretary and a sort of general clerk in the notes and discounts department. She was the one who brought you in here."

"Oh!" said Hanvey. And then—"Nice young lady."

There was no hint of humor in his heavy face, but Fiske chuckled delightedly.

"Efficient—and sour," he explained. "But mighty loyal."

"I knew she must be something."

"She was behind her desk and I had just gone out to speak with her. At about ten minutes after two o'clock the front door opened. I didn't think anything of it—a box holder, most likely. The man—"

"Remember what he looked like?"

"Only vaguely. He was slim and quietly dressed. He didn't look like a crook."

"Crooks never do."

"He walked straight up to the cage where I was talking to Miss Seward. First thing I knew about anything being wrong was when Miss Seward uttered a little shriek. I turned around and saw the man was pointing a gun at us."

"I'll bet that lady was sure scared."

"She was. Plenty. The robber was polite, but very positive. He told us to back into the vault which we have on this floor. Then he saw me looking toward the electric buttons which we have all over the place—they are police signals—and he warned me that if I made a move to touch one, he'd kill me. I believed him."

"Wise man," murmured Jim.

"He herded us into the safe and followed us. I noticed then for the first time that he carried a little black satchel. He stuffed it with all the currency we had in the safe— about one hundred thousand dollars—and then started back into the bank, I suppose he meant to take the little currency which remained in the cages. Most of it, you see, had already been transferred to the safe. And, of course, I knew he intended locking Miss Seward and myself in.

"This happened quickly—but it didn't seem quick to us. Miss Seward was crying, but he had warned her not to scream, and she didn't. The robber moved into the main part of the bank. And then—"

He paused and Hanvey prompted. "Then—what?"

"Harmon Burke came back from lunch. He's the cashier and teller. He came in the back way."

"What happened when he came in?"

"Plenty," said Fiske grimly. "First thing I knew of Burke's return was when he and the robber started shooting at each other."

CHAPTER XIV

Hanvey made a chuckling noise with his lips. "This Burke must be a real fightin' piece of furniture."

"He is. Though I never suspected it before."

"Is he here?"

"Yes. They had him at the hospital until yesterday evening. He was hit in the fleshy part of the leg. He came back this morning."

Fiske touched the buzzer on his desk and Miss Seward answered the summons.

"Ask Mr. Burke if he'd mind stepping in here."

A few seconds later the door opened and a figure entered. Harmon Burke was leaning on a cane, and, having seen Hanvey enter the bank, he exhibited no surprise at the grotesque appearance of the Gargantuan detective.

But Hanvey blinked several times. So this was the man who leaped into battle with a bank robber! He inspected the cashier with keen interest.

Harmon Burke was not at all impressive. He was a little bit of a man, scarcely more than five feet in height and of a weight which could not have been greater than a hundred pounds. Hanvey guessed his age to be in the neighborhood of forty-five; but even of that he could not be certain since the cheeks of the little man were deeply lined—whether from age or ill health, no one could tell. He had roving

gray eyes which seemed rather bright; wrists of amazing
thinness and hands which seemed too large for his body.
He wore trousers of blue serge, a stiffly starched white
shirt, a collar which was too low and of too great circum-
ference and a black alpaca coat which long since had seen
its best days.

"Harmon," said the bank president, "this is Mr. Hanvey. He's down here for the B. P. A. to look into our little
robbery."

Burke hobbled forward and extended his hand. Then,
at Fiske's invitation, he sank into a chair. The detective
regarded him in amazement.

"You and the robber fought it out?" he questioned.

Burke answered in a voice which contained a little
squeak, as though needing oil.

"Yes, sir."

"You don't look like a gun-fighter."

The little man glanced up in surprise.

"I'm not."

"But you attacked the man, didn't you?"

"Yes, sir. He was robbing the bank."

"Hmph! Tell me what happened, if you please."

"Well—" Burke was speaking meticulously. "I went out
to lunch immediately after two o'clock. I went out the
back way and used the same route back: I suppose Mr.
Fiske has explained that we always do that. I ate at my
usual place: one soft-boiled egg, two pieces of toast, a
lettuce salad and a cup of tea. I returned exactly at two-
thirty because we were to be very busy that afternoon putting up the pay roll for the Marland Mills.

"I came in the back door and saw a man putting currency into a satchel. He was holding a revolver in his right
hand. I couldn't see Mr. Fiske or Miss Seward. I immediately suspected that something was wrong."

"A rather natural supposition," agreed Hanvey. "And what happened then?"

"He yelled something at me."

"What?"

"I don't know. I didn't pay any attention to him."

"I see. . . . What did you do?"

"I jumped behind the counter and grabbed my revolver. He fired at me but the bullet struck the marble counter. He didn't hit me until I came out into the open again."

The wizened cashier spoke with the utmost matter-of-factness, as though gun battles were matters of every-day occurrence.

"You came out?"

"Oh, yes sir! I couldn't shoot at him from where I was. I ran around the corner of the counter just as he started for the front door. I fired at him and he shot at me. That was when he hit me. I was very sorry about that because I fell down and that kept me from following."

"And after you fell down?" prompted Jim.

"I fired again."

"Good Lord! After he had hit you?"

"Yes, sir. I was very lucky, too. I hit him."

"You are sure about that?"

"Quite positive, sir. You see, we found blood on the floor where he had been standing. And there was a trail of blood to the front door and across the sidewalk to the curb."

"The robber ran away?"

"Yes, sir. I regretted very much that I had not struck him in a more vulnerable spot."

"You did a-plenty. Now, Mr. Burke, what happened after that?"

The little man flushed with embarrassment.

"I fainted."

"Golly!" breathed Jim, "it was about time."

Randolph Fiske faced Hanvey proudly. "Quite a hero, isn't he, Hanvey?"

"Man! You said it! Mr. Burke, is that all you know about the robbery?"

"Yes, sir."

"Had you ever seen the robber before?"

"Not that I can remember."

"No suspicion, eh?"

"No, sir."

Hanvey rose. "That'll be all, Mr. Burke. And I'm really proud to have met you."

Harmon Burke bowed stiffly and hobbled away. When the door closed behind him Hanvey turned to the banker.

"Think of a little runt like him pullin' a stunt like that. And so far as I can figure out, he don't think he's done anything special."

"That's right, Hanvey. Burke is that kind of a man."

"His story of the gun-fight is accurate?"

"Absolutely—as far as I could see from the safe."

"What did you do while this was going on?"

"Nothing. I was frankly frightened, and, at the time I didn't even know it was Burke who was shooting. From where I was I couldn't see any one but the robber."

"What did Miss Seward do?"

"She screamed—and then fainted."

"Burke was correct in stating that the man was hit?"

"There's no question about that. There was a good deal of blood on the floor. He must have been bleeding rather profusely, too, because the trail seemed to get heavier as it approached the curb."

"He went out of the front door to the curb, eh? And then?"

"A car was waiting there for him. He jumped in the tonneau and they went off toward the east—along Archer Street."

"Anybody else see the robbery?"

"No."

"Any one see the escape?"

"No one. A negro boy who works at the gas station across the street said he heard the shooting, and he saw the front door of the bank open and the man leave. But he said he was frightened and so he ducked for cover."

"Then no one saw the robber actually drive away?"

"Yes. I did."

"How?"

"I was still in the safe. The front door was open. I saw him jump into the car."

"There was another man at the wheel?"

"Yes."

Hanvey's bulbous head moved slowly. "Same old routine. It's a wonder more of these little banks don't get stuck up."

He rose and waddled to the door, which he opened. He stood for several seconds staring into the bank, then he moved down the passageway and inspected the rear door route to Oak Street. He returned to Fiske's office, lighted another of his terrible cigars and turned kindly eyes on the banker.

"This ain't exactly going to be easy, Mr. Fiske. Except for the stick-up man gettin' hit, there wouldn't hardly be a chance for us, 'cause their program went off elegant. Now what I want to ask you is this: Leavin' the robbery itself out of the conversation for a minute—has there been anything funny goin' on around here recently? In other words, has anything happened that was unusual like strange folks snooping around, or anything like that?"

Fiske hesitated briefly. "No strangers that I've heard of."

Jim breathed heavily and blinked with exasperating slowness.

"But there *has* been something peculiar," he asserted.

"I didn't say so."

"No-o, but you kind of acted it."

Randolph Fiske was genuinely impressed. "To tell you the truth," he said, "I am sure I recognized the car in which the robber drove away."

"So-o! That sounds awful good. Whose was it?"

Fiske toyed with a blotter for a moment. "I hate to say, Hanvey. I'm afraid I've connected a series of happenings which are totally unrelated. My suspicions are probably grossly unjust."

"We ain't goin' to bother no innocent folks, Mr. Fiske."

"I hope not. Especially this one. You see, in all the excitement, I couldn't be sure it was his car."

"But you're pretty positive it was?"

"Exactly."

"Who was it?"

"A young friend of mine who is a student at the college here. Marland University. I could almost swear that it was his car which waited at the curb for the robber."

Hanvey spoke softly, and kindly.

"Hadn't you better tell me the lad's name, Mr. Fiske?"

"I guess so." The banker seemed unduly affected. "He's a nice boy, Hanvey. I've known him for three years. And I'm not positive he was driving the car. His name—" And the banker drew a long breath: "His name is Maxwell Vernon!"

CHAPTER XV

The kindly face of the banker was marked by lines of worry as though he feared he had talked too much. But the ponderous detective did not seem particularly interested. In fact, for almost a half minute he said nothing, and Randolph Fiske fidgeted uneasily.

"Vernon," remarked Hanvey finally. "Maxwell Vernon, eh?"

"Yes. They call him Max."

"Friend of yours?"

"I like him—if that's what you mean."

"What sort of kid is he?"

Fiske hesitated, then leaned forward with a sudden burst of confidence. "If I give you my honest opinion of that boy, Hanvey—will it prejudice you against him?"

"Golly, no."

"He has faults—"

"Who hasn't? Only men I'm afraid of are these goody-goody, ain't-I-honest ones. They're the cute babies! Now about Vernon?"

"It isn't a long story. You know we have a college here—I never have found out whether the town was named after the University or vice versa. Vernon entered as a freshman three years ago—he's finishing his junior year now. I met

him when he came into the bank and opened a ninety-
thousand-dollar checking account. It was rather unusual—"

"I should guess yes."

"—And naturally I had a chat with him. He's a fat
young fellow—"

"Fat like me?"

"Well, no. I'd call him pudgy. Good-natured, sunny
disposition and friendly with all the world. This money
was the remainder of an inheritance from his mother, she
having been his surviving parent."

"Orphan?"

"Exactly. In the past three years Max and I have been
quite friendly—so friendly that at times I'm afraid he has
rather resented what must have seemed like interference
on my part."

"What were you interfering about?"

"Vernon has been running through his money Pretty
fast. He started slowly in his freshman year, out the word
got out that he was very rich and he gathered around himself a group of friends rather more mercenary than genuine. He bought a snappy car and started giving parties. A
good many of the boys really liked him—although he was
pretty generally a butt for ridicule."

"I understand," said the detective as Fiske paused for a
moment. "Most folks laugh at me. There's something awful suckerish about a fat feller."

"Max Vernon is weak; about as weak as a young man
who is not vicious can be. I really believe, though, that
there isn't a vicious bone in his body. That is rather important, Hanvey.

"His first year at college he spent money lavishly. Last
year he spent it faster. This year he has run through every
cent of what little was left."

"Gosh! He *must* be a bird!"

"Too many friends for his own good. One in particular—"

"Who?"

"I'll tell you about him directly. To stick to Vernon: when I saw his money dwindling I started having sensible, fatherly talks with him. He always confessed his weakness and always promised to draw in his horns. Then the next thing I knew there'd be a walloping big check come through the bank."

"Did he have all his money here?"

"Every cent. That's why I'm in a position to know so much about him. I won't bother you with too many details. About a month ago he had run through his money. Didn't have two hundred dollars left. About a week ago he came to me and asked for a loan. I questioned him pretty closely: I was sorry for the boy, and he was desperately worried, as only a lad of that age can be. He admitted that he was broke. He said he was in a rotten fix—owed a big gambling debt—and felt that his honor was at stake."

"Does he gamble much?"

"A good deal. But that, also, I'll touch on later. He wanted to borrow money. It was his first plunge into the financial world. Of course, I explained that I couldn't lend it—at least that the bank couldn't. I did offer to lend him a trifling sum personally, but he said that the hundred dollars I offered wouldn't help a bit. He needed five thousand."

"No piker, at any rate."

"It isn't that, Hanvey. He just doesn't know anything about money . . . or if he does, he's learned it in the last month, which isn't very likely. I've seen him several times since. I've been mighty sorry for him. He always had thought that ninety thousand dollars was inexhaustible. Then, suddenly, it was gone. It took him a long time to understand that there was no more. I think the lad grew several years older in a mighty short time, and frankly, for his own sake, I was glad. He confessed to me that he had been a fool. He wanted to know what to do, and I suggested that he leave college, get a job and begin to take life seriously. His gambling debt—'the debt of honor' he rather grandiosely called it—seemed to be preying on his mind. Once or twice he even talked about killing himself, I spoke to him like a Dutch uncle—"

"You thought he meant it?"

"He meant it; yes. But I knew he'd never do it. I was merely trying to snap him out of his despondency. I wanted him to quit feeling so damned sorry for himself. All his lightness and brightness were disappearing. He was becoming moody and depressed. But there was nothing I could do about it."

"And he?"

"No one in the world could have needed or wanted money more than Max Vernon thought he did. Remember that! We might smile at his troubles, but they were pretty vital to him. The last time I saw him was April twenty-eighth when he begged me for a loan—and I again refused. He looked haggard.

"On May first, a little after two o'clock, this bank was robbed of more than one hundred thousand dollars. I am terribly afraid that Max Vernon was implicated in that holdup."

"Because you recognized his car?"

"That is only the beginning, Hanvey. When I remembered after the excitement died down that the car had looked like Vernon's, I paid mighty little attention. Then I recalled the man at the wheel—and it seemed to me that even in the brief glimpse it was Vernon."

"You couldn't swear it, though?"

"Certainly not. But I investigated, and now, Hanvey, comes the rotten part of my chain of evidence. The car

containing the driver and the robber went eastward along
Archer Street. That road passes through Birmingham. That
night Max Vernon did not return to his room in the Psi
Tau Theta house. He did not come back until late yesterday afternoon."

"Yes . . . ?"

Fiske frowned, then looked up at Hanvey's expressionless face. "I'm trying to be fair to the boy—and to you. He
went to his room at the fraternity house. But, Hanvey, there
was something else that I didn't hear until this morning."

"What?"

"He didn't come back in the car he was using day before yesterday!"

Jim blinked slowly, lighted a fresh cigar, blew a cloud
of the rancid smoke across the table, and settled his huge
frame more comfortably in the easy-chair.

"No?" he asked with depressing lack of interest. "What
did he come in?"

"A new car," said Fiske. "A brand new and very expensive one."

"Hmm . . ." Hanvey puffed thoughtfully, but said nothing. To the banker it seemed that he was not even bothering to think. Just a great human bulk occupying space.
Fiske was considerably irritated. He almost regretted the
fact that he had involved the young college student so
deeply in the robbery of two days since.

"I don't want to be misunderstood, Hanvey," he said,
with a hint of acid in his tones. "I'm fond of that boy. I
don't believe there's anything radically wrong with him.
He's weak, I admit that. Jellyfish weak. He was desperate.
I've told you everything, hoping that I've overlooked some
point which may prove to be in his favor."

"Maybe," suggested Hanvey softly, "maybe you have."

"I hope so. I don't want to see Max Vernon get into
trouble."

"Gosh!" Hanvey uncrossed his legs with considerable difficulty. "It seems like what you've told me indicates that he's in trouble enough."

"There could be worse things."

"Durned if I see how. You're fond of that kid, yet everything you've told me links him up with a bank robbery."

"I realize that." Randolph Fiske spoke in a low, strained voice. "And perhaps I'm doing him a favor."

"How?"

"Because," explained the banker, "I'd rather see Vernon convicted of complicity in a holdup than electrocuted for murder."

CHAPTER XVI

There was a brief silence, punctured by a sharp click. The banker jumped. Then he smiled. The click had been caused by the little spring of Hanvey's golden toothpick. He was toying with the dreadful implement, but otherwise did not appear unduly interested. Fiske became impatient.

"You heard me?" he asked.

"Uh-huh. But I don't exactly understand where there's any murder connected with this case."

"There isn't. But if we could prove definitely that Max Vernon helped to rob this bank, we'd pretty well clear him of the murder charge."

Hanvey scratched his head. "I'm all up in the air, Mr. Fiske. You're talking about murder, and I don't know anything about any murder. Who got bumped off, and what has Vernon got to do with it?"

"It happened at the college—Marland University—just before this bank was robbed day before yesterday. Max Vernon was arrested for the killing the minute he returned to the campus yesterday evening."

"I see. . . . Who arrested him?"

"The local police."

"Mm-hmm! They sure are hell on makin' arrests. Guess they feel they've got to keep in practice. Why did they arrest Max?"

"Because," snapped Fiske irascibly, "they thought he did it!"

"No? You don't say! I never heard the beat of that."

There was a flicker of infectious good humor in the habitually glassy eye of the detective and Randolph Fiske laughed in spite of himself.

"You *are* exasperating," he explained.

"I reckon I am. Folks get terribly impatient with me sometimes. Whose murder was Vernon arrested for?"

"A man named Thayer—Paterson Thayer. They call him Pat."

"College student?"

"Yes. I guess you'd call him that. He came to Marland two years ago and entered the junior class. He would have graduated next month. Ugly rumors followed him here. They said he had been invited to leave the two Northern colleges which he had attended. He was a picturesque figure: tall, handsome, suave, worldly—nothing collegiate about him."

"How old?"

"About twenty-three or four. The younger students looked up to him and stood in awe of his polish. He didn't mix much with the older ones."

"And his connection with Vernon?"

"That's what worries me. They became friendly from the start. Max looked up to Thayer, and I think Thayer had a supreme contempt for Vernon, but that didn't prevent the older man from bleeding Max."

"How?"

"Cards, I believe. And if any credence is to be given the rumors which followed Thayer to Marland, he was quite expert in manipulating them. Of course, Max Vernon is too kiddishly trustful ever to have suspected that he was being trimmed."

"Was he?"

"Plenty. In the past two years, Hanvey, about forty thousand dollars' worth of checks drawn by Vernon in favor of Pat Thayer have passed through this bank."

"Phew! That's real money."

"It is. Thayer must have had the technique of the professional sharper, because Vernon always seemed to think that his bad luck must change pretty soon. And it never did."

Hanvey was silent for a moment. "Interesting chap, this Thayer. Regular college hustler, eh?"

"I think so. He must have had a rather hypnotic manner because every time I suggested to Max that perhaps their two-handed game wasn't entirely straight, I found I'd stirred up a hornet's nest. He bitterly resented any criticism of his friend. And I'm sure that the five thousand dollars Vernon owed when he came to me was represented by a note he had given Thayer to cover a gambling debt."

"A hog for punishment, wasn't he?"

"I'd call it something like that."

"And it was because of this that Vernon has been arrested for Thayer's murder?"

"No-o. You see, no one but myself knows how deeply involved Max Vernon was. Financially, that is. He was arrested largely on circumstantial evidence, and because it developed that they had had a bitter quarrel on the campus less than an hour before Thayer was killed."

"About what?"

"The idea seems to be that Thayer stole Vernon's girl."

"Hmm! Nasty business. Thayer must have been an awful careless young man."

"It doesn't look good for the boy, Hanvey. Suppose, just between us, that things had rocked along as we know they have: Vernon being scientifically trimmed by an unscrupulous card sharper whom he believed to be his friend. Thayer gets all his money and a note that he can't possibly

pay. Vernon is a natural gentleman and is obsessed with
the idea that his honor is tied up in the note he has given
Thayer. Mind you, this is merely supposition."

"I savvy. Go ahead."

"Then Thayer steals the one thing left to Vernon—his
girl. Of course we can smile, but I fancy that even to a
youngster like Vernon, the loss of a lady's affections could
cut pretty deeply. But we'll go a step farther: We'll say that
it not only makes him furious, but also opens his eyes. It
makes him understand that Pat Thayer is unscrupulous. It
even makes him realize that perhaps what I have told him
is true—that luck cannot always run one way. Suppose he
gets the idea that Thayer has been cheating him at cards?"

Fiske paused for a moment and Hanvey looked up in-
terestedly.

"Durned if you ain't clever, Mr. Fiske. Lemme hear
some more."

"Taking all that for granted, then," went on the banker,
obviously pleased by Jim's approval, "we can understand
that even a chap like Vernon could go crazy. The cornered
rat, if you like; or the worm having its inevitable turn. We
do know positively that shortly after their campus quarrel
Vernon went to the fraternity house where he and Thayer
both lived and made no secret of the fact that he was bitterly angry with Thayer. A little later Vernon left the place
in his car and still later Thayer's body was discovered. He
had been stabbed in the throat."

"And even without knowing what you know about the
money situation, they spotted Vernon as the man, eh?"

"Yes. If they heard about this . . . I'm worried about the
lad, Hanvey. Maybe he killed Thayer and maybe he didn't.
If he did I'm sure it was the result of a quarrel and a fight.
The boy needs help. Looking at it one way, it seems worse
than the other. The financial bleeding, the stealing of his

girl . . . and you have sufficient motive for a young man to go momentarily crazy and kill another. From another angle, we have this same young man's loss of what must have appeared to him as an inexhaustible fortune; his desperation over finances; the five-thousand-dollar note covering a debt of honor . . . and we have a staggeringly strong reason why he must have become mixed up in the robbery of this bank. I'm afraid Vernon did one or the other, and frankly, Hanvey, I'd rather see him tied up with the robbery than the murder."

The detective lighted another cigar. There was a silence for a few minutes and then the door opened. Miss Seward shrank slightly as her nostrils were assailed by the fumes of Jim's cheroot, but she recovered sufficiently to place a card on Randolph Fiske's desk. Fiske glanced at it and passed it across to Hanvey.

"Who is John Reagan?" asked Jim.

"Chief of the Marland detective force. If you'd rather not have him come in—"

"Golly! He's the one man I'd like to talk to."

Two minutes later Reagan snapped into the room: trim and efficient. He paid no attention to the banker, but advanced on the vast bulk of Jim Hanvey.

"I want to shake hands with you, Hanvey," he said heartily. "All my life I've wanted to meet a real detective."

Hanvey grinned like a kid. "Whatcha doing, Reagan—taking me for a buggy ride?"

"I mean it." The local chief turned on Fiske. "Do you know who this feller is, Mr. Fiske? I ask you?"

"Why, yes—"

"That means you don't. He's the cops' delight. He never makes a mistake—"

"Say, wait a minute, Reagan. There's many a crook riding in limousines to-day that I should have landed. I guess

I've missed more easy ones than any man in the country. Honest, I have. But my people don't advertise the failures so awful prominent."

"Hooey!" said Reagan with hearty admiration. "And the minute I heard you were in town I followed you here. I want you to do me a favor—a big one?"

"Yeh . . . ?"

"Take charge of two cases here: the robbery of this bank and the murder over at the college."

"Man! I never fool around with killings. They're too dog-goned messy."

"You're handling this bank thing, ain't you?"

"Maybe."

"Then you'll have to take on the other."

"Why?"

"Because," announced Reagan crisply, "they're tied up tight together. I don't know how they were done, but I've got the baby who did 'em both—or knows who did. This feller killed Thayer and then came over here and copped the mill pay roll. He's sitting pretty in the cooler right this minute."

"What's his name?"

"Vernon. Maxwell Vernon."

Randolph Fiske looked pleadingly at Hanvey, and the Gargantuan detective slowly extended his hand to Reagan.

"Done with you," said Jim. "If you really want me, I'll take charge. But if I do, things are to be handled my way."

"Oh, Boy!" Reagan was enthusiastic. "Take my word for it, Hanvey—you're the boss. I won't do nothing but hang around and listen."

"Wrong," grinned Jim. "You're gonna talk—and you'll start right now."

CHAPTER XVII

"Well, that bein' the case, I'll say that I wouldn't like to be in this kid's shoes." Reagan shoved his hat on the back of his head. "I guess you want to know all the dope I've got on Vernon, don't you?"

"Sure."

Randolph Fiske started to interrupt. "I told Hanvey—"

A big, fleshy paw was raised in admonition.

"You didn't tell me nothin', Mr. Fiske."

"But—"

"I'd rather hear this direct from Reagan, if you don't mind."

"He's right," explained the smaller man. "Maybe what I've got to tell him checks up, and maybe it don't. It'll give him two angles to shoot from."

The banker nodded and Reagan proceeded.

"In the first place, it's about as easy gettin' dope off a bunch of college students as it is to get a young feller to lose all interest in girls. They'll talk all right, but they don't say much. They think they know what's important, and they tell you that—no matter what it is you're trying to find out. I've run myself ragged; but out of all the mess, I get this much:

"First, the robber was using Max Vernon's car and it's a ten-to-one bet that Vernon was driving it. Second, after the robbery occurred Vernon drove right through Birmingham and on to Steel City. I've just come back from there."

"How far is Steel City?"

"Eighty miles from Birmingham. A hundred miles from here. Roads ain't anything to brag about, though. He carried his car to a dealer and dickered for a new one on a trade-in basis. Next morning they closed the deal and Vernon turned in his old car on a new one, and paid the difference—twelve hundred smackers—in cash. Now the funny part, Hanvey, is that from all I can gather Vernon has been broke for about a month."

"What makes you think that?"

"He tried to borrow money several places—and didn't get it. They always thought that he was rich, and, of course, when he tried to borrow money the news spread pretty rapidly. Now I ask you this: If a man is dead broke one week, how does it happen that the next week he buys a new expensive car and pays twelve hundred in cash on the deal?"

Hanvey nodded. "Sounds queer, Reagan. And then what?"

"Plenty." Reagan's face was beaming with pardonable pride. "I discovered that when Vernon traded in his car, there was something missing."

"Yeh? What?"

"The floor rug!"

"Floor rug, eh? What does that mean?"

"It means this: I'm sure Mr. Fiske, here, has told you all about the robbery and how Mr. Burke and the stick-up guy pot-shotted each other. The feller must have been hit pretty hard because there was blood on the floor of the bank and a trail of blood between the front door and the curb. Ain't that so, Mr. Fiske?"

"Yes. It was rather plentiful, too."

"I'll say it was. Now, then, it's natural to suppose, ain't it, that this palooka was bleeding pretty free and easy when he piled into the back of Vernon's car.

"If it was the boy's car."

"We'll take that for granted. Anyway, he was bleeding. That blood would have gone over all the floor rug, because we got to remember that a man who has just robbed a bank wouldn't be fool enough to sit on the back seat of any car. Chances were he was curled up on the floor. Now, then, I just naturally believe it would have been common sense for Vernon and the other guy to have lost that blood-stained rug, because it would have looked pretty queer if they hadn't."

Hanvey blinked. "You ain't nobody's damfool, John Reagan."

"Thanks. Now, there's one more tie-up. I looked at the car Vernon traded in, and, Jim—there was blood right by the sills, just where it would have been left if it had run over the floor rug before the rug was thrown away. Get what that means? It proves that there was a floor rug there originally."

"Sure does, John."

"Then," interrogated Randolph Fiske hopefully, "you're positive, Mr. Reagan, that Max Vernon mixed up in the robbery of this bank?"

"The case against him looks about two hundred proof, Mr. Fiske."

"I'm glad," said the banker simply.

Reagan was surprised. "Glad?"

"Yes."

"Why?"

"Because if Vernon helped rob this bank, then he couldn't have killed Paterson Thayer."

"Oh, man! You're wrong. He probably did both."

"How could he?"

"Because he was at the fraternity house when Thayer was killed, that's how; and because they had had some sort of a quarrel just a little while before, something that almost resulted in a scrap."

"But, good God! Reagan—it isn't reasonable. You've seen this boy: does he look like a person who could murder a man and go straight from that crime to the robbery of a bank, and then calmly return to college the next day with the idea of resuming his regular life?"

"He does not," answered Reagan promptly. "But Jim Hanvey will tell you that what I'm saying is true, Mr. Fiske: You can't tell from a feller's looks just what he'll do if he gets plenty desperate. Ain't that so, Jim?"

"Yeh, John—it sure is. I've met lots of fellers that looked honest and wasn't nothing but thieves."

"You see!" said Reagan triumphantly. He produced a little notebook from his pocket and consulted its pages. "I ain't in the habit of writin' things down, Jim—but on account of this being two crimes instead of one, I tried to be mighty careful so I'd spot any alibis that might be brewing. Here's as near as I can get to the happenings of day before yesterday—May first.

"Shortly before noon Pat Thayer and Max Vernon meet on the campus. Thayer is walking with Vernon's girl. They have a row—lots of the students see it and wonder what it's all about because it seems that Vernon is one of these soft, easy-going fellers that ain't never had a fight in all the time he's been at the college. About the same time two fellers come in from classes and start wasting time on the porch of the—the—hell! I don't know how you pronounce it, but it's spelled P-S-I—"

"Psi," explained Fiske.

"—The Psi Taw Theeta fraternity house. That's a sort of college secret society like the Masons or Elks or something like that. These are a lot of crazy college kids, but pretty nice at that. There's a long tall bird with a sad face and a big mouth and lots of sense. His name is Farnum. They call him Rube; he looks it, too, until he begins to talk and then you see he ain't nobody's idiot. The other guy is his buddy: skinny little runt named Philip Gleason. I got to them when things were still hot and they gave me a fistful of real dope.

"About half-past twelve, Pat Thayer strolls down the hill from the college and enters this house. The guess is that he went right to his room, because nobody saw him anywhere else in the building. A few minutes later Max Vernon drives down the street in his car, swings in on two wheels, clamps on the brakes, climbs out and goes busting in looking sore as a couple goats. Farnum and Gleason, trying to be pleasant and chatty, call out to him that his buddy, Pat Thayer, is upstairs in his room. And then they get the shock of their lives because Vernon swings around on them and says he don't give two hoots in hell where Thayer is. Then Vernon goes upstairs, leaving my two kids goggle-eyed.

"Then, before they get over this shock, something else happens. There's a girl in school— Antoinette Peyton, and they call her Tony—who, from all I can find out, is one regular feller. This Peyton kid comes walking down the street looking not much happier than Vernon did. And she turns in at the same fraternity house. That gives the two kids a jolt because they explained to me that it's against all the rules for a girl to go anywhere near a fraternity house without a chaperon.

"But that ain't all, either, Jim; because it seems that this Miss Peyton is a dame who don't ask favors of nobody. She rambles up on the porch and asks where Pat Thayer is. They say he's up in his room and offer to call him. She says not to bother, she'll go right up. That knocks 'em for a goal, and they sit back gasping like a couple fish while she calmly starts a big scandal by walking upstairs to see Thayer. You gittin' it all straight, Jim?"

"Believe so, Reagan. You sure have found out a heap."

"Yeh—and there's a heap more. About a quarter past one Miss Peyton comes downstairs and walks away. She nods to the two kids, but don't stop for any conversation. And as far as these two are concerned, I'm sure they never went inside at all because there was a guy who don't like them sitting on the porch of another fraternity house across the street and even he swears that Farnum and Gleason never left the porch. And since he was an inquiring bird, he saw everything that happened and checked up on their stories pretty nice.

"At about a quarter before two o'clock, the two kids being so excited that they've forgotten classes, Max Vernon comes busting downstairs and stamps across the porch without so much as a Hello. He has on a different suit of clothes and there is a bundle under his arm. He beats it out to his car which is parked in the yard, heaves this bundle in the back and goes down the hill at about forty, turning in the general direction of this bank. Later I'll tell you some more about that bundle he had. Don't forget it."

"I won't," promised Hanvey.

"Fifteen minutes later Farnum and Gleason find out they're still not immune to shocks when another guy comes down the hill to the fraternity house and inquires for Pat Thayer."

"Gosh!" murmured Jim, "they must have thought he was a popular guy. Who was this new feller?"

"A professor!"

"A what?"

"A professor. And a whale of a fine feller, too. Not what you'd think a professor was, either, Jim. He only graduated

last June and before that he was the best athlete this college ever had. Believe me, I've yelled myself goofy when
that guy was playing football. His name is Welch—Larry
Welch—and, while I hate to land it on him, he's got a
pretty rotten tie-up with Thayer."

"How?"

"In the first place, this Miss Peyton who had just been
to Thayer's room is supposed to be Welch's girl. Everybody
at the college says they're nuts about each other. In the second place, Welch is the brother of the girl that Pat Thayer
and Max Vernon are supposed to have quarreled about."

Hanvey was busily engaged with his gleaning toothpick. He gave not the slightest indication of interest in
Reagan's story—but both the detective and the banker
were satisfied that he was missis nothing.

"Larry Welch remained upstairs only a few minutes,"
continued Reagan. "The boys say he looked kind of worked
up and queer when he came out and he hustled back up
the hill to the college. I don't know whether he went to
see Miss Peyton or not. In fact, there are a lot of things I
don't know yet."

"Gosh!" complimented Jim—"if you knew any more,
Reagan—there wouldn't be anything for me to do."

"Don't worry about that. But to go ahead—five or ten
minutes after Larry Welch left, the two boys on the porch
hear all hell bust loose inside. Yelling and screaming and
all, and they hear a feller coming down the steps so fast
that he's almost falling. Out on the porch comes the janitor—a wop named Carmicino. He's darn near cuckoo, but
they finally get out of him that he saw Thayer's door partly open and could see Thayer's legs. Thought Thayer was
most probably drunk—or maybe sick. Went in to straight-
en him out—and discovered that he was dead. He was still
yelling and crying when I got there."

"Who called you?"

"Either Farnum or Gleason, I don't know which."

"Everything there about as it was?"

"Yeh—all but Thayer's body. Coroner has that and they want to ship it to his home to-morrow. His sister is here to take charge. I've had the police guard at the fraternity house ever since the thing happened to see that nobody went near Thayer's room."

"And you think that Max Vernon killed him?"

"Almost."

"Almost killed him you mean?"

"I mean I almost think he did."

"But a minute ago you said—"

"That's the rotten part of this case, Hanvey. I've got too much dope against too many folks. I could convict Vernon in a minute if it wasn't for two other people."

"Who are they?"

"Miss Peyton and Larry Welch—Thayer's other visitors."

"I see . . ." Hanvey was absorbed in his toothpick. "Where are they, John?"

Reagan looked up brightly.

"They're under arrest, too," he announced pridefully.

CHAPTER XVIII

The huge detective nodded approval. "I'll hand you one thing, John—you sure have made a complete job of it."

Reagan mopped his forehead with a lavender-bordered handkerchief. "I had to, Jim. I've got those three, and I know I'm right on one of 'em.'

"Which one?"

"That's what puzzles me. One time I think it was Vernon; then I come to believe it was Miss Peyton. And just when I'm sure of that I get a hunch that it must have been Welch. Of the three, I'd rather it be Vernon."

"Why?" inquired Fiske sharply.

"Oh! it ain't fair, if that's what you mean. And what I want ain't going to convict anybody. But Miss Peyton and Larry Welch are two of the swellest young folks I've ever met."

"Would you pick Max Vernon as a murderer?"

"Out of this bunch—yes. That is, maybe. I'm durned if I know."

Hanvey was slumped in his chair, absorbedly regarding his huge hands. He spoke without bothering to look up.

"What does Miss Peyton say, Reagan?"

"Nothing. She admits visiting Pat Thayer, but that is all."

"Doesn't she give a hint as to why she went up to his room when she must have known it was against the rules?"

"No. But she admits that she knows more than she's telling."

"Of course she denies killing him, doesn't she?"

"Sure. She says they had a talk and she came away, leaving him perfectly happy and healthy. But that ain't the point, Jim: There's something queer between her and Thayer. I asked her about and she got right white—but she wouldn't say Boo. I accused her of holding something back, and she allowed she didn't care to discuss the case any further. I asked her if she had seen Larry Welch since the thing happened and she said, No. Maybe that was the truth, because the minute I found out she had visited Thayer, I had her sloughed and left orders that nobody was to visit her at the jail. I've got her in a nice, comfortable private room and she's being treated swell, but it's a cinch she hasn't talked things over with anybody since we stuck her in the cooler."

"That's good. And this chap, Welch?"

"It don't look a bit healthy for him. First of all, Thayer was running around with Ivy Welch—that's Larry's kid sister; pretty little trick just seventeen years old. She's a freshman at the University. Whether there was anything between them there shouldn't be, I can't say—and Welch won't. But even if there wasn't, and he thought there was—I reckon Welch would be a pretty bad hombre."

"Thayer was a big man, too, wasn't he?"

"Yeh, but soft. Larry could have broke him in half maybe. Anyway, it'd have been a swell scrap."

"What else you got against him?"

"Welch was the last person known to have been in Thayer's room before Mike Carmicino, the janitor, discovered the body. He seemed sore when he went to see Thayer, and he left in a hurry. Then the body was found. But even if all that wasn't enough, there's something else."

"You mean about Miss Peyton being Welch's girl?"

"Exactly. And she had been to Thayer's room before that. Let's leave the sister out of it altogether. Welch is cuckoo about Miss Peyton. Somebody tells Larry she has just paid a visit to Pat Thayer in his room, so what does Welch do but hotfoot it down to find out what the hell. Ain't it reasonable that he'd be boiling over under those circumstances?"

"Uh-huh. I've seen lots of fellers get fightin' mad at less."

"And this ain't less, Jim. There's still more. I arrested Welch the minute I could get my hands on him. I rode him down to headquarters in a taxi and had a long heart-to-heart talk with him, and all I can tell you, Jim, is that that feller lied to me like a sonovagun."

"No?"

"Yes. Absolutely. It was positively shameful, the way he lied . . . and you know as well as me, Jim, that when a suspect lies all the way through he's either in pretty deep or knows who is. Am I right?"

"Right."

Randolph Fiske was listening fascinatedly to the conversation. There was no mistaking the fact that these men were professionally thorough; but he was amazed by two things: First, their cold-bloodedness; second, Reagan's undoubted superiority of intellect. It didn't appear to Fiske that Hanvey was doing any more than listening and he didn't seem to be doing that particularly well. Fiske wondered whether, after all, he had not erred in asking the B. P. A. for aid. With John Reagan there on the job . . . why he absolutely dominated Hanvey, although it was patent that he was overawed by the big man's reputation. Fiske had seen that sort of thing before: marvelously efficient small-town doctors completely cowed by specialists of twice the reputation and not half the ability. Fiske was very keen for Reagan just then. At least, he was acting like

a detective, while Hanvey—well, Hanvey was doing nothing whatever and doing it consistently.

"When I first arrested Welch," Reagan continued, "he
blanketed everything with lies. He started off by denying
that he had been to see Thayer. I proved that up on him in
less time than it takes a goat to eat a shirt. After admitting
that, he said that he'd never been anything but the best
of friends with Thayer. Then I told him he'd better quit
lying because he was getting himself in pretty deep. I told
him there was a chance for him if was innocent because we
already had two other people under arrest. He asked who
they were and I told him. The minute I mentioned Miss
Peyton's name his whole attitude changed." Reagan paused
and chuckled. "And how!"

"Well—how?"

"He wanted to know right away why we should think
anything so ridiculous as that Tony Peyton killed Thayer.
I told him it was because she had visited Thayer's room
just before he—Welch—got there. I could see he was doing some fast thinking. He finally called me a damn fool,
which wasn't very nice, and wanted to know how Miss Peyton could have killed Thayer when he had been there after
she had gone and Thayer was alive. I put it up to him that
that wasn't a very healthy stand for him to take because
if Thayer was alive when he visited the fraternity house,
then it certainly put Miss Peyton in the clear but made it
rotten for him. I also was thinking—though I didn't discuss it with him—that it cleared Max Vernon, too; because
Max left the fraternity house before Larry got there."

Reagan stopped talking. Hanvey remained silent. It was
Fiske who could not tolerate the uncertainty.

"What did Larry say then?"

"He insisted that he was telling the truth and was willing to take the consequences. He said Thayer was still
alive when he was there, and wanted to know why I didn't

let Miss Peyton go right away. I told him I didn't believe him and he informed me once again that I was a certain kind of an idiot."

"But surely," snapped Fiske, "a man isn't going to put his own neck in a noose unnecessarily, is he?"

"Maybe," answered Reagan calmly. "Specially if he's a young fool like Welch and is crazy about a girl and thinks that she did the murder."

"Then you think he thinks . . . ?"

"Sure. About the only reason I don't believe Welch did it is because he got himself in so deep without anybody tricking him. I figure he's trying to shield some one, and that some one must be Miss Peyton. It was one or the other—"

Hanvey's soft drawl broke in.

"How about Max Vernon?"

Reagan flushed.

"Or Vernon," he amended, "The darn thing has got me goofy. As soon as I get one of them three crazy kids tied up with this, I remember something about one of the others and start all over again. The more I think the less I know and the less I know, the nuttier I get. Then the whole thing is in an atmosphere I don't know anything about—"

"Gee," said Hanvey, "you don't take me for no college man, do you?"

"No. But you ain't dumb, either. I am."

"You've done marvelously," insisted Randolph Fiske with considerable vehemence. "It seems me you've discovered everything you need to know—"

"Except the identity of the murderer," finished Reagan dryly. "Up to that point I've done swell."

Hanvey rose and waddled to the window, where his tremendous bulk almost blotted out the light. Fiske stared after him with considerable disgust. He spoke to Reagan in a guarded voice.

"Is he really good, or just a bag of wind, Reagan?"

The eyes of the Marland detective sparkled. "He's the best in the world, Mr. Fiske—make no mistake about that."

"He don't act like it."

"Sure not. But don't you ever get the idea the brain behind those tin-pan eyes of his ain't working. He knows more about this case right now than I do."

"Hmph! I think you're foolish and generous."

Jim Hanvey spoke, but without turning.

"Thayer was stabbed?" he asked over his shoulder.

"Yes."

"What sort of knife?"

Reagan shook his head.

"That's one of the queerest things in the whole case, Jim. We've looked high and low for that knife and we can't find it anywhere."

CHAPTER XIX

Larry Welch was not uncomfortable. The room which he occupied in the Marland city jail was a small, rectangular affair, scrupulously clean, and neatly—if sparsely—furnished. It contained an iron cot, painted white; a rocking chair, a small table and an unpretentious dresser. The single door opened into a corridor and the one barred window was perched up against the ceiling, permitting the entrance of light without possibility of the inmate being able to look out or get out.

The young man was lying full length on the bed when the door opened. His coat was on the back of the chair and his collar and tie were on the dresser. The white shirt he wore was open at the throat and he leaped to his feet as Hanvey and Reagan entered.

He was a fine figure of youth; scarcely more than medium height, but gorgeously proportioned. His blond hair was rather tousled and his blue eyes gave evidence of worry; but he stood squarely on his feet as though prepared to meet any emergency.

He stared with amazement at Reagan's companion. In the tiny prison room, Hanvey seemed grotesquely large and ungainly. He was mopping his forehead with a purple and white handkerchief and puffing like a porpoise. His little, fishy eyes turned protestingly toward Reagan.

"You shouldn't have done it, John."

"What?"

"Walked me all the way down here."

"Why, man, it wasn't but seven blocks."

"Seven miles, you mean. I'm all in."

The turnkey in the corridor closed the door, and Reagan performed the introductions.

"Mr. Welch—this is Mr. Hanvey; Jim Hanvey. He's in charge of this case."

The youth hesitated, but Hanvey's fleshy paw came out and Larry met it with a firm grip and a quick, friendly smile. Hanvey blinked, nodded and seated himself.

"Siddown, Welch. I'd like to talk with you a few minutes."

"Shall I go out, Jim?" asked Reagan.

"Golly! no. How about it, Welch?"

"Whatever you say, sir."

It was plain that the boy was puzzled by Hanvey. By the same token, he was reassured. Reagan seemed keen, rather hawklike. But this stranger. . . . Hanvey lay back in his chair and reached for his golden toothpick.

"You understand, Welch, that you don't have to talk at all if you don't want to. I'm just tellin' you that so you won't think I'm tryin' to put anything over."

"I understand, sir."

"I could say that anything you mentioned could be used against you. Instead I'll just say that if you're innocent, the more you talk, the more chance there is of me helpin' you. If you're guilty—well that's a gray horse of another color. And my name ain't Sir, either."

Larry grinned faintly. "I understand."

"I'll spout one thing more—and you can take it or leave it. Me and Reagan are out to find out who killed Pat Thayer and we ain't got the slightest ambition to hang something on an innocent man. Now—shall I go on and talk to you or let you alone?"

The young man seemed doubtful.

"You mean—?"

"I mean that if you want to help us, maybe we can help you. If you don't—then there ain't a bit of use wasting everybody's time."

Hanvey's tone was gentle, his manner disarming. He seemed so guileless; so transparent. Larry paced slowly up and down the room. Reagan followed him with his eyes. Jim, however, appeared to have fallen into a state of coma. Finally, the young man turned and spoke to Hanvey.

"May I ask you one question?"

"Sure, Son—sure."

"Have you spoken to Miss Peyton yet?"

"No."

"Can I believe that?"

Hanvey's eyes opened slowly. "Gosh, Son—I dunno whether you can believe it or not. We don't neither of us have to believe nothin'. But I haven't seen Miss Peyton, and that's a fact."

Larry hesitated—but only for a moment. "I believe you," he said, and then added: "I'll talk."

Jim yawned. "All right, Welch. Go ahead and talk."

"I—I'd rather that you questioned me."

"About what?"

"Whatever you want to know."

Hanvey lighted one of his obnoxious cigars and grinned at Reagan. "Maybe that ain't such a bad idea, John. What you think?"

"I guess so, Jim."

Hanvey did not look at Larry Welch. He seemed absorbed in the flight of a smoke ring he had succeeded in creating.

"You did go to see Pat Thayer at the fraternity house day before yesterday, didn't you, Welch?"

"Yes." Larry's voice was low. It was plain that he was weighing words.

"What about?"

"My sister."

"Miss Ivy Welch?"

"What was wrong there?"

"Nothing . . . that is, I didn't want anything to be wrong. I told Thayer that I preferred that he see less of Ivy."

"Did you tell him why?"

"Well, yes . . . in a way."

"What did you tell him?"

"I told him that there was too much difference in their ages. He was twenty-three and Ivy is just a seventeen-year-old kid. I was afraid she was crazy about him, and I didn't think it a very good idea to let the friendship continue."

"Were you and Thayer friends?"

"Not intimate friends—no."

"But not enemies, were you?"

"Certainly not."

"How long had Thayer been going with your sister?"

"I don't know exactly. Several months, I guess."

"Anything special happen recently?"

Larry's eyes were focused on the floor. "Nothing."

"You just made up your mind to see Thayer without anything special happening, eh?"

"Yes. When I say nothing special—I mean . . ." He rose, walked across the room, and then returned to stand in front of the huge detective. "I spoke to my sister first. I had meant to for some time—it just happened to be day before yesterday. I told her to lay off Pat Thayer and she said she wouldn't. I said that forced me to see him. And so I went to his fraternity house."

"You saw him?"

"Yes."

"Alive or dead?

Larry's eyes widened, and instinctively he drew back as though to ward off a blow.

"What do you mean?" he asked—and his voice trembled.

"Gosh! Son—I don't mean nothin'. You told me to ask questions, and I'm just doin' what you asked. There ain't no need for you to get all het up over it."

"It was such a queer question."

"Maybe so. I dunno. Of course you know he's dead now, don't you?"

"Yes," bitterly: "I understand they're holding me for his murder."

"Well, then—what would be more natural than what I asked you? It shapes up kind of queer, Son. If Thayer was dead when you got to his room, why it's a cinch you couldn't have killed him, ain't it?"

"Yes . . ."

"But if he was alive when you got there, it don't look very nice because everybody knows that you were the last person in that room before the body was found. So I ask you again: When you got to his room, was he alive or dead?"

The boy's face was white, but he answered in a level voice.

"He was alive."

"And you had a nice, friendly talk?"

"Not exactly friendly—"

"Was it a quarrel?"

"No. But then you can't exactly call it friendly for one man to call on another to ask him to stay away from a girl."

"You're sure you didn't quarrel?"

"Positive."

"Thayer didn't get sore?"

Again that strained, haggard light flashed in Larry's eyes.

"No-o . . . he didn't get sore."

"Not at all?"

"I don't know. I was only there for a few minutes."

"And there wasn't any quarrel?"

Larry whirled on his inquisitor. "How many times do I have to tell you that we didn't quarrel?"

"None," murmured Hanvey gently. "Gosh! Son—you don't have to tell me a thing. Any minute you get tired of my questions, I'll quit. I ain't aiming to get you all peeved up. And as for me asking you the same thing so much— John Reagan here will tell you I'm kind of dumb. It takes some ideas an awful long time to trickle through this fat head of mine. Now if you'd rather I wouldn't ask you no more questions—"

"I'm sorry, Mr. Hanvey. Please go on."

"Thanks, Son. And any time I step on your pet bunion don't hesitate to say so. It ain't my idea to get any man riled at me."

"I understand. What else do you wish to know about that interview?"

"Nothing."

The boy was surprised. "Nothing?"

"Not a thing. You've told me all I need to know. According to the way I understand it: Thayer was alive when you got there and you and he had a nice friendly chat— that is, it wasn't exactly friendly, but you didn't quarrel. Then you left. Ain't that the way it was?"

"Yes . . ." Larry was nonplussed. "Yes—it happened just that way."

"Good. That clears things up in my mind. Now can I ask you something else?"

"Surely."

Hanvey was staring up at the little window through which the brilliant sunlight of early afternoon was streaming.

"Do you know Miss Antoinette Peyton?"

Reagan saw Larry's figure stiffen defensively, and there was the briefest hesitation before he answered.

"Yes."

"Do you know Max Vernon?"

"Yes."

"Like him?"

"He's a nice chap."

"When you were at the fraternity house to see Thayer—did you happen to see Max Vernon anywhere about?"

"No."

"Or Miss Peyton?"

"No."

Hanvey folded his hands on his huge stomach. "You object if I ask you a personal question, Welch?"

"Go ahead."

"You're pretty keen for Miss Peyton, aren't you?"

Larry flushed. "I admire her very much."

"Nothing more?"

"I don't see . . . No, it's no more than that."

Amazingly enough, Hanvey did not pursue that topic. It seemed to Reagan that Jim was constantly coming to the verge of vital disclosures and then going off on another tack.

"Were Thayer and Miss Peyton very friendly?"

"I don't think so."

"You're not sure?"

"No."

"She hadn't ever mentioned him to you?"

"Not particularly. Just casually, that is."

"Then," asked Hanvey, "you haven't any idea why she went to visit Thayer at the fraternity house, have you?"

Larry seemed troubled. He raised his voice and spoke vehemently.

"You seem more interested in Miss Peyton than in me," he accused. "It's perfectly ridiculous to think she had anything to do with Thayer's death. She left that fraternity house before I got there. When I arrived Thayer was still alive. Therefore she *couldn't* have killed him!"

"Dog-gone if that ain't right, Son. I just plumb forgot that. I sure did."

The ungainly detective hoisted himself to his feet with difficulty. He extended one fleshy paw.

"Well, good-by, Son—and much obliged."

"You—you don't wish to ask me anything else?"

"Nope. I reckon you've told me about everything there is to tell, haven't you?"

"Why—why, yes . . . I guess so."

"Well, bye-bye, and good luck."

The door closed behind them, and Larry Welch, thoroughly bewildered and not a little ill at ease, stared at the mute panels.

In the corridor John Reagan faced his companion. He could contain himself no longer.

"Welch was lying!" he announced.

Jim Hanvey smiled.

"Sure he was, John; sure he was. But that ain't what interests me. What I crave to know is—how much? And why?"

CHAPTER XX

Summer had settled upon the Marland campus. The typical "hot week in May" afflicted the student body with supreme desuetude. The baseball and track men retained a vestige of energy. Rickety cars which had been laid up for the winter were dragged out and desperately overhauled for the perfect petting weather. And while every man and woman connected with the college was vitally interested in the Thayer killing, their interest could not very well be termed excitement.

The mercury soared to 98 every day and clung there. The numerous shade trees which lined the Bowl were exceedingly popular. Classroom windows remained open and co-eds attended lectures in the sheerest of dresses, while the masculine students dispensed with coats—a touch of informality not frowned upon at Marland.

But while the intense heat forbade any emotion so exhausting as excitement, there was no question of the fact that the campus had been deeply stirred by the killing. In particular the members of Psi Tau Theta moved about with chips on their shoulders. They were keenly conscious of the odium which had suddenly attached to their beloved fraternity, and, as a unit, they refused to discuss it. Rube Farnum and Phil Gleason, considerably subdued, had become persons of importance. A certain dignity settled upon

their shoulders, which was only proper recognition of the
fact that they had been there to see all of the preliminary
happenings and were important founts of information for
the detectives.

The students, as a whole, could not believe any of the
three suspects guilty. Tony Peyton—well, it was impossible to think that she had killed Thayer . . . although always that remark was followed by the staggering question:
"Well, then, what did she go to his room for? She knew
that would start a rotten scandal."

Larry Welch—they were less sure about him, although
it didn't seem reasonable that such a fine chap would stab
a man to death. Yet there was some mix-up that the students knew they didn't understand: Larry's relations to
Tony and Tony's to Thayer. Then there was something between Thayer and Ivy Welch.

As for Max Vernon—what unanimity of opinion there
was seemed to fasten upon him through a process of elimi-
nation. It couldn't be Tony and it couldn't be Larry; therefore, it must be Vernon! But the thought was absurd. Idea
of Max killing any one! Nobody remembered ever seeing
him angry . . . except, of course, recently—when he had
been considerably worried. It was a nasty mess all around—
the college agreed on that. And the students could be of
little help to the detectives because there wasn't one who
stuck to a theory for longer than it took him to think of
another one.

A half dozen undergrads who were lounging on the
lawn in front of the Lambda Theta Pi house, saw John
Reagan drive up in his shiny little car. They saw some
one else, too—an astounding fat man who lay back in the
seat next to the driver and complained bitterly about the
heat. Later, some one passed the word that the fat man was
a famous detective and was greeted with an outburst of
derisive laughter. That bird a detective! Ha-ha!

Hanvey snorted up the stairway in Reagan's wake. He paused for breath in the little hallway, onto which the various rooms opened. Jim was exceedingly unhappy. He announced feelingly that he was on the verge of heat prostration and refused to be comforted.

A uniformed policeman, who had been sitting in a rocker outside the door which gave access to the corner room, rose and saluted Reagan. The Marland detective nodded briefly.

"Everything inside okay, Bryan?"

"Yes, sir."

"Nobody been in or out since the killing?"

"Not a soul, sir."

"Nothing moved or shifted about?"

"No."

"Good." Then he turned to his companion. "Bryan, this is Jim Hanvey—you've heard of him, haven't you?"

"Jim Hanvey?" The policeman's eyes seemed about to jump from their sockets. "Not—"

"—Jim Hanvey himself in person. Jim, this is George Bryan of the Marland force."

Jim extended his hand. "Howdy, Bryan."

"Good Lord . . . Say, you ain't really . . . ?"

"Yes. And hot as hell. Don't you ever get fat, Bryan. It's awful in this kind of weather."

"Hanvey's in charge of the case now," explained Reagan. "What he says—goes. Pass that along to the gimmick who relieves you."

They entered the room together, leaving a pop-eyed policeman on duty at the door. Once inside Reagan stood back and curiously watched his celebrated companion.

Hanvey's fishlike little eyes looked everywhere and appeared to see nothing. After all, there didn't seem to be much to see. It was a corner room, with four windows: two of them opened toward the south and two toward the east. There was a brass bed, a dresser, an old-fashioned chiffonier;

an ancient easy-chair upholstered in leather, and one straight chair. Opposite the foot of the bed was a bookcase partly filled with textbooks and modern novels. In the corner stood a set of golf clubs and two tennis rackets. There was a second door in the room and Hanvey opened it. It was a hanging closet filled with clothes which were undoubtedly expensive both as to material and tailoring.

Reagan waited for Hanvey to do something—and was disappointed. Jim merely stood in one spot, breathing audibly and mopping the back of his neck. But finally he turned, and Reagan prepared for a pronouncement of importance.

"One thing I'm sure of," said Hanvey.

"What?"

"I never have felt no hotter weather!"

It was Reagan who was forced to remind Hanvey that they were supposed to be working on a murder case. With some little display of pardonable pride, he directed Jim's attention to certain chalk marks on the floor.

"Who made those, Reagan?"

"I did."

"What for?"

"They outline the position of Thayer's body as it was when I got here. That straight line where you're standing is the mark to show how far open Carmicino says the door was when he spotted the feet of the body from the hall."

Jim nodded approvingly. "Fine work, John. I never could understand how you detectives manage to think of all those things."

"Quit kidding, Jim."

"I ain't kidding: on the level, I ain't. Now me—I'd have come in here and looked the body over and remembered how it lay. But I never would have been positive sure after that because it would just have been my memory. I can see now. . . ."

He opened the door and stepped into the hall. The door itself hung just over the straight line which Reagan had marked. Jim stood in the middle of the hall and looked. From the spot he could see that section of the chalk marks which denoted the position of Thayer's feet and ankles.

"That's what Carmicino says he saw, Jim. He thought Thayer was most likely stewed and so he went in the room. Then he found out the man was dead and started yowling."

"I see . . ." Hanvey walked back in the room and Reagan followed, closing the door again.

"Did you look over his papers?" asked the fat man.

"Sure."

"Find anything?"

"I think so. I found his bank book for one thing. It's in a Birmingham bank—not the Marland one. He's deposited some large amounts and there ain't much question that he was getting them from Max Vernon."

"Any other deposits?"

"Yes. Some small, and others as high as a couple of hundred dollars. But there isn't any record of where they came from."

"Any letters?"

"A few."

"From girls?"

"Plenty. Especially from Ivy Welch—Larry's sister. Want to read 'em?"

"Mushy?"

"I'll say. And how! The kid was crazy about that bird and no mistake. He was her first love and all that sort of thing. There wasn't anything in the world she wouldn't do for him. They were plenty hot and funny."

Jim Hanvey was staring into the sunshine beyond the closed windows; there was a queer, soft light in his usually expressionless eyes.

"I reckon I won't read 'em, John. I never could get a whale of a laugh out of love letters."

Reagan flushed. He knew Hanvey hadn't meant to rebuke him . . . but, by Gosh! who ever would have suspected that mountain of flesh of being a sentimentalist? John fidgeted awkwardly, and Jim dropped a kindly hand on his shoulder.

"Forget it, John. It's just that I'm queer about some things."

There was an awkward silence, which Reagan broke.

"What now, Jim?"

"Now? Golly! I dunno. What do you reckon I ought to do?"

Again Reagan felt baffled. There were moments and this was one—when he believed Hanvey was superbly stupid.

"Would you like to see Farnum and Gleason? They're the two boys who were on the porch when all this stuff was happening."

"No-o. I reckon not."

"Don't you want to talk to Mike Carmicino? He found the body, and he has worked in the fraternity house for several years. I guess he knows a lot about Thayer and Vernon both."

Jim's eyes lighted, as though at a new and very pleasing idea.

"That's a swell thought, John. Where'll we find this janitor?"

CHAPTER XXI

They located Mike Carmicino in the basement of the fraternity house. He gazed with somewhat startled surprise at Hanvey's disconcerting bulk, and then conducted the two detectives to his room—a small, rather untidy cubicle in a corner of the basement. Reagan explained that Hanvey was in charge of the case and wished to question him . . . then there was silence for several minutes during which the swarthy janitor eyed the expressionless countenance of Hanvey with growing wonder and bewilderment. When Jim did speak, his tone was quiet—almost a whisper.

"You were here all day on May first, Mike?"

Carmicino's face beamed.

"Oh, yes, sir. I was nowhere else at all."

"How long have you worked here?"

"I have been janitor five-six year maybe."

"Of course you knew Mr. Thayer pretty well, didn't you?"

Carmicino made an expressive gesture. "I know him very good. He is one fine feller."

"And Mr. Vernon?"

"Also he is a fine feller, Meester Hanvey."

"Do you know Miss Antoinette Peyton?"

The black eyes of the janitor danced with enthusiasm. "I know her good. She is—"

"Sure. She is a fine feller. I understand." Jim produced his golden toothpick and toyed with it. "Was Miss Peyton in this house the day Mr. Thayer was killed?"

"Yes, sir; she was here."

"What time?"

"I don't know very good, sir. I have a wrist clock, but she do not run very often."

"You saw Miss Peyton?"

"Oh, no, sir. I did not see her. Not any."

"Then how do you know she was here?"

Mike grinned engagingly. "Because all the fellers they say she go up to Meester Thayer's room."

"Hmm! But you did not see her?"

"No, sir. Not even one time."

"Have you ever heard of her coming here before?"

"Oh no, sir. Ladies, she do not come to fraternity house."

"Did you see Mr. Vernon on May first about half-past one o'clock?"

"Yes, sir."

"Where?"

"Upstairs."

"Doing what?"

"I see him doing two things. First I see him go into Meester Thayer's room, and long time beyond that I see him leaving the house."

"You didn't see him leave Mr. Thayer's room?"

"No, sir."

"Where were you when you first saw him?"

"I was cleaning hall on the second floor."

"That was when you saw him go into Thayer's room?"

"Yes, sir."

"Did you notice anything queer in the way he looked? Anything different from his regular expression?"

Carmicino looked away and shook his head. "I not know how you mean expression, Meester Hanvey."

"No-o? Was Mr. Vernon mad?"

"How I know was Meester Vernon mad? I cannot say was he mad or was he happy. He go into Meester Thayer's room, but always he do that on account those two fellers is very fine friends forever. No, Meester Hanvey—I cannot say was Meester Vernon mad because I was just cleaning hall and I do not know."

"You like Mr. Vernon?"

"Oh! I like him many."

"Did he ever give you money?"

"Mooch money. He gives big tips."

"You wouldn't like to see him in trouble, would you?"

"No, sir—I do not be happy to see Meester Vernon in trouble."

"And so you wouldn't likely remember if he was mad or not?"

Carmicino's black eyes narrowed as they flashed to the face of the detective.

"I would not say something about Meester Vernon I do not know, Meester Hanvey. If I know he is mad, I say he is mad. If I only see his face, I not tell you I guess he is mad, because Meester Vernon he is always nice to me."

Hanvey nodded approvingly. "Fine boy, Mike. You and I ought to get along great. Now, you say you saw Vernon leave the fraternity house?"

"Yes, sir, I see that."

"Where were you?"

"I was work' downstairs—back of the house—when I see Meester Vernon come down before he leave."

"Was he in a hurry? Was he walking fast?"

"Yes, sir—he come down the steps pretty fast."

"Do you remember if he had anything in his hands?"

"Not in his hands, no, sir. But he have a bundle under his arm."

"What sort of bundle?"

"I don't say for sure, Meester Hanvey; but I think from where I was work', it look like a bundle of clothes."

"Do you remember if he was wearing the same suit when he left the fraternity house that he had on when he entered?"

Again Carmicino hesitated. When he answered it was as though honesty was distasteful. "I feel mos' sure he was not wear' the same suit."

"You think he changed clothes between the time he visited Thayer's room and the time he left the house, eh?"

"I think, yes. But I do not know for sure."

"Do you know Mr. Larry Welch?"

"Yes, sir. He is one fine feller."

"Did you see him on May first?"

"No, sir, I do not see him any."

"You didn't see him come to this house or leave it?"

"No, sir. I do not see him at all. Of course I hear everybody talk that he have been here to see Mr. Thayer. But me, I don't set even one eye on him."

"Now, suppose you tell me what happened after Mr. Vernon left the fraternity house?"

Carmicino rose. He walked slowly up and down the room punctuating his words with large gestures.

"I was work' in the back downstairs when I see Meester Vernon go away. I do lots of work back there: sometimes in the kitchen, sometimes down in the cellar. Always I do not stay on that floor. Then I get my mop and floor wax and go up to second floor. I do not see anybody when I go up there, so I start waxing the floor and after 'while I look over and I see Meester Thayer's door is a leetle bit open. I do not pay attention to that much, except when I look again and I see his foots and also his legs, and I think right

away it is funny he should be lying down on the floor—because that is funny thing to do.

"Then my mind says to me that maybe Meester Thayer,
he is drunk, and I think I will put him on the bed so he
can sleep it away. I do not want the other fellers to know
Meester Thayer is drunk in the fraternity house because
that is not nice except when they have a party. I walk to
the door . . ." The chunky frame of the janitor seemed to
shrive at the remembrance and there was a wild light in his
eyes: "I go in the room, Meester Hanvey, and right away
I see that Meester Thayer he is not drunk, because his
throat—his throat . . ." The janitor covered his face with
his hands and rocked back and forth. "He is all blood,
Meester Hanvey. I touch him once, and I see he is entirely
dead and then, Meester Hanvey, something take hold of
me—here—and I get frighten' scared and I do not know
anything more until I am downstairs with Meester Farnum
and Meester Gleason and they are say, 'What's the matter,
Mike?' And that is all, sir—because anything else I do not
remember because I am so afraid when I see that blood."

Reagan relaxed as the story finished. He had heard it
before from the expressive lips of the janitor, and it stirred
him peculiarly. He glanced now at the prodigious detective to see what effect it had made. Hanvey was lying back
in his chair with eyes half closed, apparently oblivious to
everything. The little room was poorly ventilated: the air
was hot and close. It was a setting to add drama to Carmicino's recital . . . yet, for all the interest he exhibited, Jim
Hanvey might not have heard.

Reagan wanted to break the awkward silence, but dared
not. Carmicino stared curiously at the bovine Hanvey,
then sank into a chair, his sharp, black eyes roving about
the little room. And when Hanvey spoke, it was in a casual—almost disinterested voice; and about something else.

"Who did you like best, Mike—Vernon or Thayer?"

Carmicino did not hesitate.

"Meester Thayer, sir. I like him most best."

"Why?"

The swarthy face turned brick red, but the man did not evade.

"I like Meester Thayer best, sir, because I feel like him and me, we are partners."

"Huh? What you mean: Partners?"

"I mean . . . I do not like to say this, sir, because you are policeman, but I promise to tell the truth. Meester Thayer and me, we do much business with each other."

"What sort of business?"

"Whisky."

Reagan sat up very straight. This was something entirely new to him. He heard Hanvey's soft, reassuring drawl.

"You mean," asked Jim, "that Thayer was a bootlegger?"

Carmicino made a gesture of horror.

"Oh no, sir. Meester Thayer, he is one fine feller. He only get the orders and I buy the whisky for him. It is me which are the bootlegger." He paused for a moment in obvious embarrassment, and then made a further explanation. "But I am not common bootlegger, Meester Hanvey. I get whiskey only for the college fellers, and always I am careful that it is good stuff."

CHAPTER XXII

Jim Hanvey appeared to be absorbed in the mechanism of his patent toothpick. His eyes were focused on that device when he spoke again to Carmicino.

"Are you a regular bootlegger, Mike?"

"Oh, no, sir. I would not do nothing like that—only for the college fellers." The janitor's eyes flashed to Reagan's stern face, then back to the more placidly reassuring countenance of the sleepy Hanvey. "I hope I do not get to jail because I tell you that, sir."

"You won't," promised Hanvey. "Will he, Reagan?"

"Whatever you say, Chief."

Hanvey pursued his inquiry. "How was this liquor thing worked, Mike?"

"It was theesaway, Meester Hanvey: Always sometimes the boys give a party which the faculty they do not understand about, so they want liquor. Meester Thayer, he is on the committee, and he says he knows where he can get real stuff which has never been cut. So they give him the money and he orders from me."

"I see. . . . And you and he would split the difference, eh?"

"Yes, sir. For real thing, the fellers they pay me one hundred dollars a case. I pay for it sixty dollars a case, and Meester Thayer he takes twenty dollars and I take twenty dollars."

"Then you were close friends, eh?"

"Oh, no, sir. Meester Thayer, he is ver' fine gentleman and he would not be friends with no janitor."

"I see. . . . He certainly was a fine gentleman, Mike—no mistake about that." The little eyes moved restlessly. "Gosh! ain't it hot?"

"Rather step outside?" suggested Reagan.

"No. Might as well stick here for a minute or two." He turned to the janitor again. "Thayer and Vernon were pretty good friends, weren't they?"

"Oh, yes, sir. They was buds."

"Did you ever hear them quarrel?"

"No, sir. Not one time even."

"They used to play cards a good deal, didn't they?"

"Maybe so—maybe not. I think maybe so."

"Vernon never mixed up in this liquor business, did he?"

"No, sir. Just Meester Thayer."

"Hmm! When was the last time you bought liquor for him?"

"Let me see . . . about one week ago, sir. It was a nice party. They wanted two cases."

"Two hundred dollars' worth?"

"Yes, sir."

"Did you get it?"

"Oh, yes, sir."

"Did Thayer pay you for it?"

"Right away quick, sir, all except the forty dollars which he keep for himself."

"He always looked after you, didn't he?"

"Yes, Meester Hanvey; always he sees that I get my money ver' quick so the man from which I buy it off, he also does not be force' to wait."

"Did Thayer usually pay you when he ordered the whisky or only after the boys paid him?"

"After the fellers they pay him. You see, it is for them and so he should not pay me until he get the money from off them."

"And when he died, Mike—did he owe you anything?"

"No, sir. Meester Thayer, he did not owe me one cent."

"Good." Hanvey hoisted himself to his feet, and nodded to the janitor. "That'll be all, Mike."

"You do not ask me no more questions?"

"Nope. Nothing else. I'm much obliged for everything."

"Thank you, sir."

Reagan led the way into the hall and thence upstairs to the main floor. Several boys, having heard that a new detective was on the case, were gathered on the veranda, struggling to appear disinterested. But all eyes were directed at Hanvey's ungainly figure as he and Reagan stood at the foot of the steps chatting.

"What now, Hanvey?"

"I dunno, John. What you reckon?"

"Would you like to see Max Vernon's room?"

"You've searched it, haven't you?"

"Yes."

"Find anything?"

"Not a thing. But I thought—"

"My Gosh! you're a thorough bird. Well, let's go. But Lordy! how I hate those steps."

Hanvey panted to the top floor and Reagan conducted him into a small but handsomely furnished room, resplendent with pennants, pillows, tennis rackets and numerous lithographs depicting pulchritudinous damsels in various conditions of deshabille.

But despite the markedly collegiate tone, there was more than a hint of taste in the general arrangement. In a corner was a delicate statuette perched on a teakwood tabouret. And over the mantel was a collection of curious weapons: A fencing foil, a broadsword, a Malay kris, an

Arab scimitar, a rusty revolver of Civil War days, a Philippine bolo, a bow and arrow of genuine Indian origin. Hanvey glanced at them, and then at the arrangement of the room.

It was cozy, in a youthful, happy-go-lucky sort of way. Hanvey casually opened the dresser drawers and rummaged indifferently through the masses of expensive linen. He opened the door of the hanging closet and exclaimed over the multitude of tailored suits disclosed.

"Vernon sure must be a snappy dresser, John."

"Looked that way to me," answered Reagan enviously. "I always did wish I could afford them kind of clothes. I'll bet there ain't a suit in yonder that cost less'n a hundred bucks."

Hanvey walked to the window and stared off toward the sprawling town of Marland. Midafternoon, and most classes were finished, so that the shady spots under the trees were peopled with male students and co-eds. They seemed to be doing nothing whatever and doing it with enthusiasm. Jim sighed.

"I used to think I missed a lot by not going to college, John. Now I know it."

"Don't they have it easy? Just sitting around under the trees and talking to girls . . ."

"I wish I was young again—and not so durn dumb. Somehow, John, I never could knock any book stuff into my fat dome. I'd study the idea and it'd sort of die before it reached my brain. But man! I'd sure have been a whale at this laying around stuff."

Hanvey sank into a chair and lighted a cigar. "Ain't it tough to think of a kid like Vernon having it easy like he did and then getting mixed up in a nasty mess like this?"

"You tell 'em, Jim. That's one reason I was glad to get you on the case. They're a nice sort, these kids. I didn't used to think so. I thought they were a bunch of crazy high-hats, but, by golly! they ain't. I haven't met a one who didn't strike me that he'd be a real guy if he wasn't so dam' educated."

Hanvey moved his head laboriously toward the mantel.

"What's all the military equipment?"

"I asked about that," said Reagan. "It seems Vernon has traveled a good deal and he's sort of collected these things. That funny-looking one is from where the Malays live. I think they call it a kris. And that one over the clock is a bolo, or whatever it is the Filipinos use. Vernon was a nut about 'em."

"Funny hunch . . . But at that I guess it's more sensible than collecting stamps or art things." He blinked. "You've looked all through the room, John?"

"Everywhere. I'm sure I didn't miss a thing."

"You never can tell. . . . Just to make sure, though, we'll make one more search."

Hanvey did not move and Reagan stared at him uncertainly.

"What do you mean, Jim: *We?*"

"We?" echoed Hanvey. "That means you, John. I'm a rotten searcher."

Reagan started with the dresser. He rummaged through the drawers and into every corner. He inspected every ornament and spot of dust on the mantel. He looked behind pennants and pictures which were tacked to the wall. He opened the door of the hanging closet, where he commenced a systematic search into every pocket of every suit of clothes.

It was a tedious job and Reagan—glancing occasionally into the room—was quite sure that Hanvey's suggestion for a new search had not been entirely without ulterior motive.

The prodigious body was settled snugly into the big chair; the pudgy hands were folded contentedly across the massive mezzanine and Jim Hanvey was—or far as the naked eye could discern—sleeping superbly.

Sleeping! Or was he? The longer Reagan was with Hanvey the less he understood the big man. At times he appeared to be obtuse, at times brilliant and at times just plain dumb. Reagan returned his task. If Hanvey wanted a search he'd darn well get one. Reagan had been over every inch of ground before . . . but he was determined to do this second job as thoroughly as he had the first.

And then the silence of the room was shattered by a sharp cry from the closet. Hanvey's eyes uncurtained slowly, but he exhibited no other excitement—even when Reagan leaped into the room holding something gingerly between his thumb and forefinger.

"Good God, Chief—look here."

Jim eyed the trophy curiously.

"Dog-gone . . . It's a knife. And there's blood on it, too. Where'd you find it, John?"

"In the corner of the closet. On the floor. I—I don't understand, Jim—because I looked there day before yesterday. . . ." He was more excited than he cared to show. "But we've got something here, Chief—no matter if I did overlook it before. With this, it ought to be plain sailing."

"How come, John?"

"Because," snapped Reagan triumphantly—"that is the knife that killed Thayer, and, Chief—I've got another idea."

"Good for you, John. What is it?"

Reagan stepped swiftly to the mantel. He designated a spot on the wall where the papering was of a lighter color.

"Unless I'm all wrong, Hanvey," he said—"this knife belongs right in that spot. And if it does—there ain't much question but that Max Vernon is the man who used it."

CHAPTER XXIII

Hanvey deigned to become interested. He and Reagen regarded the weapon. It was a powerfully delicate thing and beautiful as a poisonous snake.

The handle was of polished metal, whether nickel or silver, neither knew. The guard was exquisitely carved, and the blade, which was unusually long and perilously keen, was of the finest tempered steel. At the moment it was not a pretty sight, however, for the steel was covered with blood which had clotted almost to blackness. Hanvey moved away, leaving the knife lying on the table.

"I hate to look at anything like that, John."

"I don't."

"You're hard-boiled."

"Oh, hell! it isn't that, Jim. But I like to find something when I'm on a case which means I don't have any farther to look."

"I see. . . . I reckon that's natural, John." Hanvey placed his hands behind his back. "Where'd you find that?"

"On the floor of the hanging closet—in the corner."

"Didn't you look there day before yesterday?

"Sure I did."

"Yourself?"

"Yes."

"I thought you said there wasn't anything there?"

"I did, Jim; but I suppose I overlooked it. Though I'm darned if I see how I did."

Hanvey shrugged. "Those things can happen, all right. It's queer, though. . . ."

"What?"

"Nothing . . . I was just thinking."

Jim seemed disinclined to comment further, and Reagan did not force him. As a matter of fact, the chief of the Marland plainclothes force was elated. He was annoyed that he should have overlooked so valuable a clue on the occasion of his initial search, but now that he had found it . . . "It's like you told Randolph Fiske, Jim—a dick can make a dozen mistakes provided he does the right thing just one time. The crook can't afford to slip once."

"True enough, John. You sure don't get any argument out of me. But it is funny you didn't see that knife when you first looked in the closet."

Hanvey rummaged around in a dresser drawer until he found a collar box. He emptied this and then waddled into the bathroom, from which he returned with a roll of absorbent cotton. He lined the collar box with cotton and then gingerly placed the knife in the box. But he did not immediately look up. His eyes were fixed steadily on the weapon.

"Funny," he said at length.

"What?"

"The handle of that knife, John—it's polished metal, and yet there isn't a fingerprint on it."

"Well, I'll be . . . durned if you ain't right."

"What you reckon—?"

"Cinch. Max Vernon had enough sense to polish the prints off the handle."

"You sure think fast, John."

Reagan looked up sharply, but the face of the fat man told him nothing.

"D'you think I'm wrong?"

"Gosh, no! Seems like you must be right. It just looks kind of funny, though, that you didn't find that knife day before yesterday."

Reagan was disturbed. He was certain that he had looked in that identical spot the afternoon of the murder, and he had found no knife. His brain was racing, and suddenly he whirled on his companion.

"I've got it, Chief."

"What?"

"The answer to that knife. First, there's the off chance it was there all the time and I just didn't find it. I hate to admit that, but it's possible. The second theory is that Max Vernon had it with him and when he came back yesterday evening from Steel City he dumped it in there before I stuck him under arrest. He was in this room when I grabbed him."

Hanvey's big head nodded slow approval. "Now you're talking, John."

"You think I'm right?"

"It sounds mighty reasonable. Question is, are you sure it is Vernon's knife?"

"We'll ask him—that's one way of finding out. And in the second place, look at that spot on the wall. It's like this, see—" Reagan stepped to the mantel and removed a scimitar which hung there. "Notice how you can see on the wall paper just where this hung, Jim? Dust couldn't land right underneath it, and it makes the paper look lighter. Yonder is the place the dagger was hanging—it fits that spot exactly. And you can tell it's a foreign thing."

"Ain't any question about that. It sure don't look awful healthy for Mister Vernon."

"It don't—and I'm sorry. I believe the kid has gotten a lousy deal all 'round. This Thayer evidently wasn't a thing but a plain, high-class hustler. He probably sized up the

college when he first got here and picked Vernon as his
meat . . . and made a darn good pick. It's a cinch that he
must have been trimming him at cards, and we know that
he was gypping his fraternity brothers on the liquor game.
Of course, Carmicino thinks Thayer was a fine gentleman,
but he would think that. As a matter of fact, Thayer was a
dud and we both know it."

"We sure do."

"But that don't make Vernon's position any happier. He
quarrels with Thayer about a girl. We know that Thayer
had trimmed him good and plenty. We know that Vernon
was desperate for want of money. We know that he went
to Thayer's room and that shortly afterward Thayer's dead
body was found. Now we locate the knife with which he
was killed. We find it in Vernon's room and identify it
positively—or will pretty soon—as being part of Vernon's
collection of weapons. We have every reason to believe
that the kid went plumb loco and took part in a bank
robbery because he was desperate. The robber probably
made a deal with him that all he had to do was drive a car,
figuring no one would ever suspect a college student's car
in a college town, even if it was hitting sixty on the road.
We're sure Vernon was mixed up in that because we know
he didn't have a thin dime before the thing happened, yet
the very next day he buys a new car and pays the difference
of twelve hundred dollars in cash. And I also know that
he has lied like the devil about everything since I put him
under arrest."

Jim whistled softly. "It sort of makes Mister Vernon
out to be a pretty tough hombre, John."

"He isn't that. I just think he went nuts."

"Maybe so. . . . But he sure stayed crazy a long time."

Reagan was a trifle annoyed. It did not please him to
have his damning summary greeted with even the slightest
semblance of skepticism.

"What's wrong with my case, Jim?"

Hanvey arched his eyebrows in surprise. "Golly, John! I didn't say anything was, did I?"

"No. But you looked funny."

"I can't help it if I look funny, John. A guy who has a face like a custard pie and a shape like a goldfish bowl is entitled to look funny, ain't he?"

"But," accused Reagan, "you don't really think it was Max Vernon!"

"Who says I don't?"

"Do you?"

"Pretty near."

"What do you mean: Pretty near?"

"Well—" Hanvey drew a long, audible breath. "I sort of just happened to remember Larry Welch."

"Yeh? What about him?"

"Vernon had left the fraternity house before Welch got there, yet Welch says that he had a long talk with Thayer. Now it sort of seems to me, John, that if Thayer was already dead, Larry would have noticed it, wouldn't he?"

"Hmph!" Reagan was crestfallen. "I think Larry lied."

"Why?"

"To shield Miss Peyton. He's goofy about her."

"You're right. . . . But then if he's sticking his own neck into a noose to shield her, don't it strike you that he's got some mighty good reason—a reason we don't know—for thinking that she killed Thayer?"

"I know, Jim—but we've got Vernon dead to rights. He's bound to have done it—"

"Provided neither Larry Welch nor Miss Peyton did."

Reagan frowned, then broke into a disappointed laugh.

"You win, Jim. I kept running into snags like that all the time. That's why I wanted to pass the buck to you." He eyed the big man keenly. "What's your idea about the thing?"

"I haven't had an idea in a month. They don't come to me swift, like they do to you."

"But you surely think something?"

"Yeh—true enough. And the first thing I think, John— is that I ain't hardly talked to anybody about this affair. Until I see some of the others, I won't know where I stand—"

"And after you do see them, you'll be absolutely bughouse. I know . . . believe me, I do."

"I'll try, anyway."

"Who first? Vernon?"

"No-o. I think I'll have a chat with Ivy Welch."

CHAPTER XXIV

Reagan conducted Hanvey to the office of the Dean in the Main Building. Dr. Boyd was startled by Hanvey's appearance and appeared somewhat skeptical of the man's ability, but he was courteous—and readily acceded to Hanvey's request that Ivy Welch be summoned.

"It's rather a ghastly affair all 'round, Mr. Hanvey," he said, "and I do hope you'll be able to solve it satisfactorily."

"Yes, sir." Jim was visibly awed by the atmosphere of education which pervaded the unpretentious office. "I sure do. But I wonder what you mean by 'satisfactory'?"

The Dean smiled slightly. "My personal preference plays a prominent part in that, Mr. Hanvey. I should certainly hate to see either Mr. Welch or Miss Peyton become any more deeply involved."

"And Vernon?"

"I like the boy—make no mistake about that. But he doesn't seem to be of the same fine quality as the other two. Of course, some one killed Thayer—"

"Uh-huh, Dean. It sure seems so."

Dean Boyd looked up sharply, rather suspecting subtlety in the words of the detective. But the man's face was so heavily blank, and his manner so inert, that the Dean concluded he was totally lacking in intelligence. Just why a smart, alert person like Reagan should serve under an oxlike creature of Hanvey's type was beyond the Dean's comprehension, but then he never had understood the police very well, anyway.

The door opened and a figure of vivid youth entered the room. Ivy Welch looked particularly dainty and unusually pretty this afternoon. She wore a white, sleeveless dress and a short, revealing skirt. The Dean introduced her and then excused himself, promising Hanvey that they would not be interrupted.

While he bowed himself out, Ivy stood eyeing the two detectives. There were high spots of color in her cheeks and it was obvious that she was not at all frightened. But she showed the effects of the terrific shock to which she had been subjected. Tragedy—grim and stark—had invaded her life early, and left her peculiarly matured. There were dark circles under her eyes, to tell the story of tearful, sleepless nights—and she twisted her hands nervously. When the Dean had gone she addressed Hanvey with courageous directness.

"Are you in charge of this case now?"

"Yes, Miss Welch—I guess so."

"Well, I'm glad. This man here"—she jerked her bobbed head toward Reagan—"is absolutely dumb."

"Is he, really?"

"I'll say he is. Else why would he keep my brother in jail? Anybody could talk to Larry and see that he isn't the kind who would kill anybody. That is, anybody but a cop!"

Hanvey turned gravely to his companion.

"You see what the public thinks about you, John."

Reagan grinned. "Yeh! But didn't I tell you first off that I was a little vacant upstairs?"

"You did. And seeing that we don't need any solid ivory around here—suppose you run along and let me talk to this young lady alone?"

"Very well." Reagan rose, without resentment, and started for the door. Hanvey followed. He spoke in guarded tones. "Just had a hunch I could do more with her alone, John. She looks like a little fighter, and if she is sore at you, she'd be scrapping every minute. Suppose you take this knife down to the jail and ask Vernon if he's ever seen it before."

"And then?"

"Come back and come in. I got a hunch she and I will be pretty good buddies by then."

Reagan marched off and Hanvey reentered the Dean's office, closing the door behind him. He liked the trim little figure—although she somewhat frightened him. She was sitting now in a straight chair, and her legs were crossed—disclosing a frank expanse of pink flesh between the knee and the hem of the dress. Hanvey felt himself blushing, but Ivy seemed totally unconscious of her display.

He settled comfortably in the Dean's swivel chair, popped his forehead and the back of his neck, and then grinned disarmingly at the girl.

"Answer me one question, Miss Welch: Ain't I the terriblest looking detective you ever saw?"

The girl's blue eyes opened wide and a truant dimple appeared. "Well, I wouldn't say you were a sheik."

"I ain't this bad in cold weather. Heat just knocks me for a row of tin cans. Now Reagan yonder . . ." He lowered his voice. "You mustn't get sore at regular dicks, Miss Welch," he advised confidentially. "All they know is to run around arresting everybody who could have been mixed up in a crime . . . and then sort of weed 'em out. See?"

"I see. And it's thoroughly stupid."

"But easy, Miss Welch—easy. In fact, I might say—a cinch. If they slough everybody, they're bound to have the right one. Me—I don't hardly ever make an arrest, and my

job now is to turn loose at least two of the three Reagan
has got in stir." Jim was using police vernacular in a deliberate effort to impress the girl, and he knew that he was
succeeding. She was sitting forward tensely; completely
awed by his authoritative manner. "One thing, Miss Welch:
I want you to know I'm on the level. I wouldn't try to put
nothing over on you—cross my heart and hope to die if I
would. If you don't believe that, why, there ain't hardly no
use for us to talk."

"I think you're all right," said Ivy firmly.

"Thanks. It's real nice of you to say that. And now that
we've started off so good, lemme tell you one thing more: I
ain't a regular bull. I ain't got the slightest desire to make
a record, and I'd rather never slough anybody than do any
harm to the wrong feller. You're sure your brother didn't do
this thing. I sort of agree with you. But there's a whole lot
of lying going on . . . and while I don't want to make you
sore, Miss Welch—it ain't any secret that your brother is
doing more than his share—which ain't helping him a bit."

"He would!" snapped the girl.

"—To shield Miss Peyton: sure he would." Jim spoke
casually and apparently did not see Ivy's start of surprise.
"I want to locate somebody who knows something and is
willing to talk straight. Will you or won't you?"

Ivy didn't hesitate. "I will!"

"Good girl. Now I want you to tell me about Mr. Thayer—and yourself . . . just whatever you feel I should know."

The girl bit her lip. "I feel funny about that, Mr. Hanvey.
I've tried to tell one or two people—even my brother—and
they all laugh—or sneer when I say I was in love with him."

"I wouldn't laugh, Miss Welch. I'm a sentimental old
bird . . . and I believe in young love. Gosh! how I do."

"I'm seventeen," she said. "I guess I'm not so awful
dumb. I know about as much as the next girl. And I was in
love with Pat Thayer. Not crazy about him—just in love.

There's a sort of a difference: I mean, when a girl is crazy about a boy it's one thing, but when she's in love with him it's something entirely different. And this was different."

"I get you. I sure understand, Miss Welch."

"He was wonderful to me. Not always wisecracking and showing off smart like most boys. He was awful different, and I guess a girl knows whether she's in love or not, no matter how much people laugh. And when he—when he—" Her eyes filled with fierce hot tears which she dashed away. "I'm an awful silly little fool, Mr. Hanvey—but I can't help it."

"You go right ahead and cry, Ivy." Hanvey's voice was infinitely gentle. "I guess I know how you feel. Once when I was a heap younger—and a heap thinner—I had a girl. And I lost her. . . . She married another feller, and it sort of seemed as though she had died."

Ivy sensed the very genuine sympathy and the deep human understanding. The campus tragedy had hurt more than any one suspected. There had been the shock, the horror . . . then the fear that Larry might have done it. Only her roommate knew of the long hours of crying . . . only the roommate could tell of the heroism which sent Ivy Welch bravely out on the campus. But Ivy had not talked to that roommate. Hanvey, now—he was different. She felt that he understood, and would help. It was a relief to talk. . . .

"Pat Thayer and I were engaged," she said simply.

"Gee . . ."

"Of course, we weren't thinking about getting married just yet. We both felt I was too young. But I was wearing his fraternity pin and he was wearing a diamond ring which used to belong to my mother." Again her eyes filled with tears. "He had it on when—when he died, Mr. Hanvey."

Jim shook his head. "Where is it now, Miss Welch?"

"I don't know. I suppose it's still on—on his finger. I put it there myself."

She suddenly buried her face in her hands. Hanvey, filled with a deep pity, watched her in silence. Then the blonde head jerked upward and she forced a smile. "I won't talk about it any more, Mr. Hanvey. I'll try to be a good scout. I know it don't make you feel good for me to act like a baby."

"You go right ahead, Ivy. . . . You've had a rotten time and I reckon you and I are the only ones who know it."

The girl's starry eyes turned on him.

"You're going to help get Larry free?"

"Yes—if he is innocent."

"Surely you don't think . . . ?"

"No, Ivy—I don't. But I do think that Larry has talked himself into a lot of trouble. And if he won't tell the truth it's up to me to find it out from some one else."

"I'll tell you everything I know."

"Good. Now first: Weren't you with Mr. Thayer day before yesterday just about noon?"

"Yes, sir."

"Did Max Vernon meet you?"

"Yes, sir."

"What happened then?"

She hesitated, and her cheeks grew white; but she answered with brave honesty:

"They had a pretty nasty quarrel, Mr. Hanvey."

CHAPTER XXV

Hanvey leaned forward. "Would you mind telling me, Miss Welch—what Vernon and Thayer quarreled about?"

She flushed slightly. "About me."

"Why?"

"Well," she answered with a flash of the straight-for-wardness which he liked—"I guess I acted pretty rotten. I had a date with Max and I stood him up."

"I see . . . You preferred being with Thayer?"

"Of course."

"Why?"

"Because Max is just a kid. He's a good sport and all that, but he's a baby."

"Haven't he and Thayer always been good friends?"

"Yes."

"When did you notice any change?"

"Oh, I can't just remember, Mr. Hanvey; but Max has been impossible lately. Mooning around with a face like last week's wash, and always talking serious instead of kidding along like he used to. I got awful bored. Then I started going with Pat—that's Mr. Thayer—and Max got sorer than ever. He bawled me out about it three or four times and I said I'd go with whoever I wanted. Then he asked me for a May Day date. I was to eat lunch with him in the cafeteria and we were to go to the class track meet. I met

Pat and just naturally forgot the date—that's all. Then when Max met us he got nasty about it, and, of course, Pat wouldn't stand that."

"Of course not. What did Mr. Thayer do?"

"Oh, he sort of treated Max like a kid. Max got awful sore. I mean, he was downright ugly about it."

"And then?"

"He stalked off, trying to look like a man."

"And you and Mr. Thayer?"

"We talked for awhile and then he said he had to get ready for an afternoon class. He said if Max was sore and wouldn't take me to the track meet, he'd take me."

"That was nice. . . . Now, about your brother . . . ?"

Her eyes flashed. "You know he wouldn't kill anybody, Mr. Hanvey. You've met him: he's a fine man . . . and he just wouldn't do anything like that."

"Did you see Larry between the time Thayer left you and the time Larry went to see him at the fraternity house?"

She looked away, and he could see her fingers clasping and unclasping nervously. Jim leaned forward and touched her hand. "Please be honest, Miss Welch. If I don't get the truth from some one . . ."

"Yes. I saw him."

"Where?"

"Over at the women's dormitory. He came to see me."

"What about?"

Her answer came in a whisper. "Mr. Thayer."

"I see . . . What did he say about Mr. Thayer?"

"He said—he said I wasn't to see Pat any more."

"Why?"

"He wouldn't tell me. There's always been a lot of mean talk around the campus about Pat. He was better than the rest of them and they all hated him for being more of a man. And Larry knew of it—"

"Hadn't he known of it for a long time?"

"Why yes."

"And he knew you had been going with Thayer, didn't he?"

"Sure. I never made any secret about it."

"Then why did he suddenly come and speak to you day before yesterday?"

Again her cheeks turned white. "Somebody had told him something."

"Yes . . . ?" Jim was infinitely patient. "Who?"

"Antoinette Peyton."

"I see . . . And how did Miss Peyton happen to pick that particular day to tell him?"

"Because—well, it happened this way, Mr. Hanvey." She walked to the window and motioned him to join her. "You see, all the college buildings are on a hill here. Then there's the athletic bowl and another hill beyond. Way over yonder on that big hill is the women's dormitory. When you walk over there you go down the hill beyond the Bowl and pass through a pretty little patch of woods. There's a place down there all kind of closed in—everybody knows it. It's called the Bower and couples there lots of times. It's a sort of college rule never to go in there when some one else is there. I mean not to go in when you hear somebody.

"Tony Peyton was coming from the dormitory and Pat and I were in there. It was being there with Pat that made me forget my date with Max Vernon. Anyway, Tony Peyton eavesdropped and then busted right in on us. She—she gave Pat the devil."

"For what?"

"For making love to me."

"I see . . . But what business was it of hers?"

The face which Ivy lifted to Hanvey was a study in bewilderment.

"I don't know!"

"Didn't she say?"

"No. Of course I could tell that there was something between Tony and Pat; or, anyway, there had been. Tony was awful sore, and Pat was mad. He told Tony to mind her own business and that if she butted in on him she'd be starting something she couldn't stop. Tony said he ought to be ashamed of himself because I was such a kid, and he said he'd do what—what he damn pleased."

"And you?"

"I just stood there. It seemed like I was an outsider. I hadn't ever seen Pat mad, and I never thought Tony could get so sore."

"It was a real fuss?"

"Yes, sir. I think Tony must be crazy about him, and she was jealous. Anyway, I mean she acted just like that."

"You didn't get any hint—from either Pat or Miss Peyton—what there was, or had been, between them?"

"No, sir."

"And you think Miss Peyton told your brother that he ought to do something about it?"

"Yes . . . Larry is crazy about her."

"Did he give you any hint—about Miss Peyton and Thayer?"

"No. Larry didn't act nice. You'd have thought he was my father instead of my brother. He said I'd have to quit going with Pat. I said I wouldn't, and he said he'd see that I did."

Jim's eyes were half closed. His voice came in a slow, disinterested drawl.

"And then he told you he was going over to see Thayer, didn't he?"

"Yes, sir."

"That was about half past one?"

"I think so."

"He was real sore when he left you, wasn't he?"

She seemed startled. "Not sore enough to kill anybody, Mr. Hanvey. Don't you understand: Larry isn't that kind at all. Maybe he could have quarreled with Pat and had a fight . . . although I never have known Larry even to do that. But anyway, he could have beat Pat up. He never would have used a knife."

"Do you know if he and Miss Peyton are engaged?"

"I don't think so. I mean, I think Larry would like to be, but I'm sure Tony was crazy about Pat Thayer."

"Mmm! Did you tell your brother that you and Pat were engaged?"

"Sure I did."

"Did you mention that Thayer was wearing your diamond ring?"

"No. I just didn't remember. I wasn't scared to tell him, though."

"I don't believe you were . . . Tell me: Would Larry have been likely to recognize that ring? Did he know it pretty well?"

"Yes, sir. It was my mother's."

"Larry went to see him to make him stay away from you. He was mad when he went. Yet you think he didn't kill Thayer?"

"I'm sure of it, Mr. Hanvey. You know, you can imagine a person doing some things—and there are some things that a certain sort of person just *couldn't* do. Larry couldn't stab a man. Any one would tell you that."

"They have," admitted Jim. "And they've told the same thing about Miss Peyton and Max Vernon." He rose ponderously. "I'm much obliged, Miss Welch. You've been a darn good sport and you've helped me a heap."

She rose and faced him, and for a second a womanly dignity seemed to have settled upon her.

"Will you tell me the truth about one thing, Mr. Hanvey?"

"Sure pop."

"It's this: Have I helped my brother or hurt him?"

Jim smiled a broad, lazy smile.

"You've helped him, Ivy. I give you my word on that. You see, for the first time I got a little of the truth."

He watched her as she opened the door. He saw her give a start, and her slim figure stiffened.

"You!" she cried sharply.

"Yeh, it's me," answered Reagan from the hallway.

"You've been listening!"

"No'm, I haven't. Honest. I've just been waiting for Jim Hanvey."

Ivy withered him with a glance and stalked off down the hall. Reagan entered the room grinning.

"Any luck, Jim?"

"Plenty."

"Got any hunches?"

"Yeh."

"Against who?"

Hanvey chuckled. "Everybody," he answered. Then: "Did you see Vernon?"

"I did."

"Show him the knife?"

"Yep"

"What did he say?"

"He said," answered Reagan, "that the knife is his!"

CHAPTER XXVI

They spoke briefly to the Dean and left the building together. Below them was the Bowl: long concrete stand on either side, cinder path circling the diamond; men in track suits loping easily around the oval or practicing field sports; the regulars indulging in a practice game against the freshman baseball team. Under the trees were a half hundred cars; some empty, some occupied by youthful couples; the stands held perhaps a hundred students and through the woods one could glimpse couples—usually of mixed gender—walking slowly and talking earnestly.

It was a quiet, peaceful scene: a scene which made a profound impression on the Brobdingnagian Hanvey. He was fascinated by the informality of it. His idea of college had been so different: earnest, spectacled young men and women studying aggressively; a general air of stiffness and studiousness. But this . . . why, they actually seemed to like it. He gazed upon the young folk with real envy and there was a feeling that he had missed something in life—something which he would like to go back and take. He expressed all this haltingly to his companion and Reagan looked at him in amazement.

"What the hell would you do with a college education, Jim?"

"I dunno. . . . It ain't the education, John. But when I look at this sort of thing I get a hunch it ain't what's written in books that these kids take away with 'em. Maybe I'm wrong, but it seems I'd sort of like to look back on four years of this kind of stuff."

"Yeh! and all they're thinking about is finishing up."

"P'raps. I ain't saying they ain't. But, by golly! a few years from now they'll look back on this . . . Oh, hell! there I go getting mushy again. Fine big stiff I am to yearn for an education at this late date."

"You said it!" muttered Reagan. "Me, I never have thought college amounted to much."

"No—I reckon maybe it wouldn't—for you. I'm just a softy."

They circled Old Main and slowly descended the hill toward the Psi Tau Theta fraternity house where Reagan's car was parked. Students eyed them curiously and buzzed with conjecture. Hanvey was relaxed. He was thinking—and Reagan was bitterly disappointed because he didn't seem more excited about his disclosure regarding the ownership of the knife which had been used to kill Paterson Thayer. He was even a trifle hurt, though he wouldn't say so. He attempted to elicit a comment from Hanvey—and went at his task circuitously.

"You and the kid seemed to get along fine, Jim."

"Ivy Welch? Say, she's a regular, John."

"Darn little cat if you ask me. Did everything but scratch my eyes out."

"You don't say. I reckon she must have a weak spot for a poor old fat feller like me."

"Ten to one she didn't tell you anything."

"Gimme the ten, John. She told me plenty."

"What?" Doubtfully.

"We-e-ell, she said that she and Pat Thayer were engaged. Thayer and Max Vernon quarreled just before

Thayer was killed. Thayer and Miss Peyton had a run-in because he was shinin' up to Ivy Welch. Then Ivy and her brother had a row, and he left her with the intention of seeing Thayer and ordering him to lay off."

"She knew we had all that dope already."

"Maybe she did, John—and then, again, maybe she didn't. Anyway, it was refreshing to get it from somebody who ain't accused of this killing. Allowing for the fact that she'd maybe try to shield her brother, I don't think she's got a thought in the world except to help us catch the person who really killed Thayer." His eyes closed slowly. "She sure was in love with that guy."

"Kid stuff!"

Hanvey turned slowly and regarded Reagan for a minute.

"I think that's the same mistake everybody made when they thought of her in connection with Thayer. All they said was: Kid stuff."

Reagan's eyes narrowed.

"What you driving at, Jim?"

"Nothin' special. Just ramblin' in my speech, as usual. Only remember this, John—when a girl of seventeen falls in love, it ain't kid stuff to her, no matter what it seems like to other folks. I think maybe everybody would have done better to realize that Ivy Welch was a woman grown. Get me?"

"No!" exploded Reagan, "I don't. What do you mean?"

Hanvey shrugged. "Durned if I know," he confessed. Then: "So Max Vernon admitted that was his knife, eh, John?"

"Yes."

"Did he see the blood on it before he made that admission?"

"Hell, no, Chief. I ain't that dumb. I had the blade covered when I showed it to him. I asked him if he'd ever seen it before and he said, sure, it was his. I said: 'You

couldn't be mistaken about that, could you?' and he said
he certainly could not. Then I told him he'd put his foot
in right, because that was the knife that killed Pat Thayer
and I showed him, the bloody blade."

"And what did he say?"

Reagan shook his head. "He said he didn't give a damn
if it had killed Thayer or not, he didn't have anything to
do with it. I asked him how come his knife was used, and
he said it was my job finding out things like that. He's a
darn fresh kid, Jim—and he hasn't told the truth about
anything since I first stuck him in the hoosegow. Let's go
over and have a talk with him. What say?"

"Not yet, John."

"Where shall we go?"

"Let's go to the undertaker who's got Thayer's body. I
want to take a look at it."

"Come ahead." Reagan stepped into his car and Jim
crawled in on the other side.

"Any of Thayer's family down here?" asked Hanvey.

"A sister. Seems to be a pretty nice sort, but she won't
talk much. I got a hunch that he was always a sort of bad
egg, Jim. And, of course, a feller can't press that kind of
an investigation too strong with a man's sister when he's
lying dead in the next room."

"Gosh, no." They turned into Marland Road and sped
along under the spreading shade trees which lined the pav-
ing on both sides. "John," asked Hanvey suddenly, "when
you searched Thayer's room did you find any jewelry?"

"Nothing but a watch and chain."

"No diamond ring?"

"Sure not. What gave you the idea?"

"I just thought . . . You're sure there wasn't any diamond ring lying in that room anywhere? Not in his trunk
even?"

"There wasn't!" said Reagan crisply. "Just because I overlooked Max Vernon's knife you haven't got any right to think I'd miss that sort of stuff everywhere."

"Aw, now, John—don't you go gettin' peeved at me. I just asked you a question friendly-like, and—"

"I ain't peeved, Jim. But dog-gone it! You seem to have more ideas and less words than anybody I ever saw."

Jim chuckled. "Don't you mind me, Kid. I'm just dumb, and the less I say the smaller chance there is of any one finding it out."

John Reagan laughed.

"Kid yourself, Jim—if you want to," he said. "But don't try to kid me."

At their destination, the undertaker conducted them into the cubicle where Thayer's body was being held under police orders. Hanvey grimaced with distaste and made no secret of his dislike for the job in hand. He was frankly frightened by the sight of death, and didn't even look at the body as Reagan gave a clinical dissertation on the killing.

". . . right in the neck," he was saying and the voice came to Hanvey as though from a distance. "The doc says it severed the jugular vein which is why there was so much blood. I asked him would it need to have been stuck by a person with any strength and he said, no, in that spot the slightest shove of a keen knife would do the work, and the wound itself shows that the knife was keen. Clean wound, you see."

"Yeh . . . Ain't that sweet?"

"I asked him if a woman could have done it, and he said, sure, a child could have."

"You haven't got any children under suspicion, have you, John?"

"No. Say—what the devil . . . Well, anyway, he hadn't told me much because even if he had said it would have

been strength I wasn't forgetting that Antoinette Peyton
has been a big athlete in this college. Strong, see? Then I
asked the doc—"

"Tell me that later," suggested Hanvey hastily. "I want
to get out of this place quick."

"Good Lord, Jim—if you didn't want to look things
over, what did you come here for?"

"To find that diamond ring."

Reagan fell back a step.

"I don't know what you're talking about. That's twice
you've cracked about a diamond ring."

"Sure," murmured Jim. "Sure I have. It seems right important."

"What does?"

"The diamond ring. You see, John—at the time Pat
Thayer was killed, he was wearing a diamond ring which
Ivy Welch had given him. I want to see if he's still wearing
it."

Reagan bent over the body. When he straightened his
expression was one of complete bewilderment.

"You sure you got your dope straight, Jim?"

"Yeh."

"Then there's something darn funny—because Thayer
ain't got anything on his fingers except a signet ring with
some foreign letters on it."

Hanvey turned reluctant eyes on the body.

"It's gone all right, John."

"I'll say it has." Reagan's forehead was creased with
intensive thought. Suddenly he smashed his right fist into
the palm of his other hand. "And you know what it means,
Jim—that diamond ring being gone?"

"What does it mean, John?"

"Just this: Thayer was alive when Larry Welch went to
see him. Larry saw the ring and knew what it meant. He
had it out with Thayer and killed him. Then he took his

sister's ring off Thayer's finger, because he knew if he left it there it could be traced back to her. Am I right?"

"Durned if I know, John. But whether you are or not, you sure sound reasonable."

CHAPTER XXVII

The Marland jail bulked forbiddingly against the full moon of a perfect May night. It was a not unhandsome structure, as jails go; but it frowned sternly upon the sprawled-out, pretty town as though to say: "It is because I am so grim that you may live here safely." Citizens of Marland were proud of their jail: of its staunch concrete walls, of its marble portico, of the heavy iron bars which proclaimed to an erring world that it would do well not to err here.

Jim Hanvey, somewhat stupefied by the effects of the dinner with which John Reagan had plied him, stood at the curb and commented in complimentary fashion on the building, thereby bringing a thrill to the heart of the local detective. Then they walked through the big gates and thence to the warden's office. The big man was to have access to the prisoners at any time. The warden, somewhat reluctant to believe that this uncouth man-mountain was the Hanvey of whom he had heard, nodded dumbly and conducted the two men to the little room which was occupied by Antoinette Peyton.

She rose as they entered: a trim, graceful, womanly figure in a dark blue dress. She showed signs of the strain: there were faint circles under her eyes and it was plain that she was making an effort to remain calm. When she spoke her voice was subdued, and her manner that of hostess rather than prisoner. Reagan introduced Hanvey and all three seated themselves; Tony in a chair beneath the tiny window, Hanvey and Reagan on the bed.

"You understand, Miss Peyton," said Hanvey quietly, "you don't have to talk if you don't want to."

"I have no objections to talking," she answered calmly.

"Good. I shall have to ask questions which might be kind of—well—direct. Is that all right?"

"Yes."

He liked her cool, quiet, straightforward manner. It was as though she had nothing to hide and nothing to fear. The big man reached for the golden toothpick and clicked it open. It seemed impossible for him to talk unless his pudgy fingers were busy with that ghastly instrument.

"I'm not going to waste your time with a lot of silly questions, Miss Peyton. I reckon I could start at the beginning and check up with you on all the things I know already just to see if you'd tell me the same story. But I won't."

"Thank you," said Tony gratefully.

"I'm only going to ask you about those things that nobody else can tell me." A broad, engaging grin split Jim's lips. "That's fair enough, ain't it?"

"Yes. . . ." She found herself warming to this big man. He seemed honest: genuinely, deeply honest.

"I know," continued Jim softly, "that you overheard a sort of love scene between Mr. Thayer and Ivy Welch. You butted in, and a general row followed. It don't matter just what was said. The point is that you and Thayer and Ivy were all sore, weren't you?"

"Yes."

"Now the first important thing I've got to find out is this, Miss Peyton: What was your relationship to Pat Thayer? What I mean is: What right had you bawling him out for making love to another girl?"

Tony's face flushed, and, for an instant, her eyes flashed. She answered rather coldly:

"I think you're presuming a good deal, aren't you, Mr. Hanvey?"

"No, ma'am. Honest, I ain't as dumb as I look. I know there was something between you and Thayer. Maybe it was jealousy—maybe something else. But it's awful important that I find out."

"Why?"

"Because if I don't know the truth, I've got to figure things my own way. You see, that's a sort of link in the chain that's got to be welded. There's a heap about this case I don't understand . . . and one of the most important things is what there was between you and Thayer."

"I don't see. . . ."

"I'm sorry if you don't," pleaded Hanvey, "because it ain't helping nobody for you not to tell me the truth. Even if I know the truth it couldn't hurt you any worse than having me think things. That is, unless you really killed him yourself—"

"Good God!"

"I didn't say you did. But listen, Miss Peyton: Put yourself in my place. What do I find out: You run across Thayer making love to a pretty little blonde. You give him thunder—and it's clear there's something between you. At the end of that interview you're threatening each other. Then a little later you do something that I bet no other girl has ever done since Marland was built—you walk straight up to Thayer's room in the fraternity house and a little while after you leave they find him dead. Could the real truth hurt you much worse than that?"

Tony rose and walked the length of her cell. Then she stood in front of Jim Hanvey and gazed intently into his round face and kindly gray eyes.

"I feel that I should speak frankly. I—I have a hunch that you're not trying to trick me."

"Thank you kindly, ma'am. And you've got me right: I swear you have."

She bit her lip, then spoke sharply. "You are wondering how I dared to go to Mr. Thayer's room in the fraternity house when I knew it would start the whole campus gossiping, aren't you?"

"Yes'm."

"You know that I knew it would set off a nasty scandal?"

"Yes."

"And therefore you know I had a good reason for going there?"

"That's it, Miss Peyton. Because no matter what you went for, or what happened after you got there, it was a cinch that you were going to start the whole campus talking."

"That," announced Tony bravely, "is precisely why I went there."

"To start gossip?"

"Just that."

"Why?"

"So the truth would come out, and when it did, Pat would be forced to let Ivy Welch alone."

"The truth? What is the truth, Miss Peyton?"

Tony did not evade. Her answer came in a firm, cool voice:

"I am Pat Thayer's wife!"

Jim blinked and fumbled for his toothpick again. There was an audible gasp from John Reagan. And then, as they listened in stupefied silence, Tony told—in a level, emotionless tone of how she had happened to marry Pat Thayer and of what had occurred since that time. When she finished she seated herself, limp and frightened. Suppose she had done the wrong thing? Suppose . . . her eyes quested hungrily for Jim Hanvey. He seemed so comfortably friendly. There was something in his solid calmness which compelled one to avoid evasion. One gathered that he instinctively knew truth from falsehood; that he respected the former and despised the latter. The girl took a deep breath. Her brain told her that she had erred; instinct said that she had done the best thing.

"And so you see," she said, after the long pause, "I had to protect Ivy. I knew Pat Thayer was married—but she didn't."

"I see. . . . And, of course, you were not jealous, were you?"

"Of him?" She gave a short, bitter laugh. "He is dead now—and this may not sound well: but I despised him."

"That explains a good deal. . . ." It was as though Hanvey were talking to himself. "Of course, no one could be expected to guess that you were Thayer's wife. And nobody else knew it, did they, Miss Peyton?"

"No. . . ." The color flooded her cheeks.

"You mean: Not then?" prompted Hanvey.

Reagan's head jerked up sharply. He saw the girl start with surprise. He saw her cheeks blanch. Then he looked curiously at Hanvey. The big man seemed totally disinterested. He was gazing fondly at the gleaming toothpick—apparently unmindful of the vital question he had asked. Reagan had just concluded that Jim didn't even know what he had stumbled upon when Hanvey repeated his question in a quiet, conversational tone:

"Even Larry Welch didn't know then that you were Thayer's wife, did he?"

And now Tony Peyton was defiantly on guard. Her tiny fists were clenched and she was sitting forward tensely.

"No," she said sharply. "He didn't know."

"But," suggested Jim, "you told him a few minutes later, didn't you?"

"Who says I did?"

"Gosh! Miss Peyton—I didn't say anybody said so. I was just asking: that's all. And please don't get all worked up. You'd think I was trying to trap you. I ain't: honest, I ain't."

"But you said—"

"I just suggested that you went straight to Larry Welch and told him the truth. Ain't that a fact?"

"I think I'd rather not discuss it any more, Mr. Hanvey. I'm afraid I've already said entirely too much."

Jim didn't argue. He rose ponderously and bowed with a queer courtliness.

"That's all right, Miss Peyton. I promised you I wouldn't try any police tricks on you, and I won't. I'm trying to help, not hurt, and I can't help unless I get the truth. But I ain't advising you to tell me a thing you don't want. So me and Mr. Reagan will say much obliged—and good night."

He moved toward the door. Reagan, inwardly seething at Hanvey's stupidity, followed reluctantly.

And then, as Jim opened the door, the girl spoke.

"Wait. Please."

"Yes, Miss?"

She faced them bravely. "I suppose I'm a fool," she said. "But I believe I can trust you. If you don't mind staying a little longer, I'll be glad to tell you the whole truth."

CHAPTER XXVIII

Even yet Hanvey did not press his advantage. Reagan was fighting to restrain his own impatience—and meeting with little success. Here was the big chance: an opportunity to gather important facts from a woman who had been locked up for two days and was willing to talk.

But Reagan was a good sport. If he didn't understand Hanvey's slow, friendly, ponderous methods, he could at least follow them since he himself had offered the case to the fat man. They seated themselves once more and Tony spoke in a brittle voice.

"What is it first, Mr. Hanvey?"

"We-e-ell, I don't rightly know. Suppose we start with your visit to Larry Welch. What did he say when you told him you were married to Thayer? Was he surprised?"

"Certainly."

"Sore?"

"No-o, I wouldn't say that exactly. The thing seemed to shock him."

"Did he say anything about seeing Thayer?"

"Yes. He wanted to go right over, but I begged him not to."

"Why?"

"Because I wanted to see Pat first."

"For what reason, Miss Peyton?"

"Because . . . well, there's another detail we left out. Larry and I had meanwhile discussed Ivy, as I remember it. He was quite determined that Pat should not go with Ivy any more. I had a right to seal his lips about my marriage to Pat, but I had no right to say that he shouldn't keep him from going with Ivy. So I asked him not to go over until I had seen Pat myself."

"Why?"

She met Jim's kindly eyes levelly.

"I was afraid."

"Of what?"

"A fight. Pat Thayer was a big man. Larry is perhaps more powerful. So far as I know, Mr. Thayer was not a coward, and no man can very well permit another to order him away from a girl without—well, without resenting it."

"I see. . . . And why were you afraid of a fight?"

"Because of the scandal," she answered promptly. "That sort of thing would be certain to leak out, and it would have been very embarrassing. You see, Larry is an instructor here. He is about to earn his Master's degree. It wouldn't have been nice. . . ."

"You weren't afraid of any serious results—that is, physical results?"

"No. Of course my sympathies were all with Larry, and I knew he could handle Mr. Thayer."

Jim focused his eyes on the toothpick. "You are in love with Larry Welch?"

Her cheeks grew white, but she did not evade.

"Yes."

"Does he know it?"

"Yes."

"How long has he known it?"

"I think he has known it for a long time, but I didn't put it into words until—until day before yesterday."

"I see. . . . Day before yesterday Larry learned that a married man was fooling with his kid sister. He learned that you could not marry him because you were married to another man—the same man. He learned of the petty blackmail which Thayer had practiced on you. It makes a rather damning lineup, doesn't it, Miss Peyton?"

"Yes. And I've told it to you straight because I believe Larry is innocent."

"I hope so. . . . Now would you mind telling me what happened when you went to see Thayer at the fraternity house?"

"I went there with a definite object in mind, Mr. Hanvey. He knew the minute I walked into his room that his hold over me was gone. A girl cannot visit a man's room in a fraternity house without starting all kinds of gossip. I told him that I had done that so I would have no choice but to announce our marriage. You see, I felt that I could spike his guns that way."

"For what?"

"So that he'd have to drop Ivy Welch—or else she would drop him. And that would make it unnecessary for Larry to interfere."

"You were still afraid of what might happen between Larry and Thayer?"

"Yes—and I regretted having told Larry. But things happened so fast and I had been under such a strain for so long a time. . . . I—I just wanted some one to talk to."

"While you were in Thayer's room . . . ?"

"He was furious, of course. We quarreled bitterly. I suppose I was as angry as he was. And then I left."

"Where was he when you left, Miss Peyton?"

"Standing near the dresser."

"Alive?"

She caught her breath sharply. "Of course. . . . Surely you don't think . . . ?"

"I had to ask you that. I'm sorry." Jim inserted a cheroot between his pursy lips and puffed meditatively upon the unlighted atrocity. "Did you know that Larry Welch has been arrested?"

"Yes. . . ." She spoke almost in a whisper.

"Do you realize that everything you have told me serves to incriminate him?"

"Yes." She flung her head back. "I don't believe the truth can hurt anybody. I know Larry didn't do it, just as I know that I didn't. I've told the plain, straight truth, and that's all. It's what Larry would have me do."

"It isn't what he has done," said Jim softly.

"What do you mean?"

"He hasn't been honest with us."

"He couldn't be. He gave me his word that he wouldn't tell anybody I was Pat Thayer's wife."

"He didn't tell us any untruths about that, Miss Peyton: he simply kept his mouth shut. It was on something more important."

"What?"

"He says that when he left the fraternity house, Pat Thayer was alive."

"And why isn't that the truth?"

"I can't tell you *why*, Miss Peyton, but I am saying that I am sure it is a lie."

"You have no right, Mr. Hanvey, to think—"

"No-o. I reckon I haven't. But we promised to be honest with each other, didn't we? I'm just playing my end of the game as fairly as you played yours. I can't tell you why I think it, but I'll bet my right hand that when Larry Welch left that fraternity house, Pat Thayer was dead. And Larry knew it!"

She did not indulge in dramatics. She merely sat very still and her body seemed to get cold as ice. She stared at the huge figure opposite.

Hanvey met look for look. And she, searching the moonlike face for a vestige of reassurance, saw nothing but grim honesty.

"Then," she gasped, "you think Larry killed him?"

"I can't say that, Miss Peyton," he amended gently. "I believe that he lied when he said Thayer was alive when he left. And now I know why."

"Why, then?"

"To shield you. He had just learned your secret, knew—probably—that you had been to see Thayer. And if he didn't kill Thayer, then he found the body when he got there and thought you had done it. It's a situation as old as romance. But at any rate, it was a pretty fine thing for him to do, because by his own admission Thayer was alive while he was there, which makes it certain that he must have done the killing."

"Larry didn't do it, Mr. Hanvey. I *feel* that."

"So do I. But if he didn't—who did?"

She shook her head. "I don't know. . . ."

"It wasn't Larry, you say."

"He couldn't do a thing like that—even in a fight."

"It wasn't you."

"Is that—is that a question, Mr. Hanvey—or a statement?"

The big man smiled slightly. "I don't know. Do you?"

"I didn't kill him."

Hanvey rose and shook his head. "This ain't any cinch, Miss Peyton. If I'm to believe what I hear: you didn't kill him and neither did Larry Welch. It almost looks like if I carry the investigation far enough I'll find out he ain't dead." Suddenly he started forward: "I'm sorry, Miss Peyton. I didn't mean to crack any bum jokes. Honest, I didn't. I'm just a damned blundering jackass."

Out in the courtyard of the jail, John Reagan turned admiringly to his companion.

"I'll hand it to you, Jim: you're a marvel. But how in hell do you do it?"

"Oh! I dunno, John. Shooting square with 'em, maybe. And maybe it's because they look me over and decide I'm so dam' stupid I wouldn't understand a lie if I heard one."

"Hmm. . . . And now?"

"What do you think, John: Welch or Miss Peyton?"

"Neither," snapped Reagan. "It was Max Vernon, just like I said at first. You gave me an idea back yonder. It happened this way, and I'd bet a nickel on it: Tony Peyton went there just like she said. Then Vernon went to Thayer's room and killed him—not meaning to kill him when he went in, maybe, but doing it in a fight. Larry Welch gets there a little later and finds the body. Thinks Tony did it. Pulls the hero stuff. What do you think of that?"

"Sounds reasonable," commented Jim guardedly. "Anyhow, I reckon there ain't any objection to lettin' Welch and Miss Peyton out on bond, is there?"

"None whatever," agreed Reagan. He rubbed the palms of his hands together. "I feel like we're getting somewhere at last."

"So do I," grinned Jim Hanvey. "The thing I am puzzled about is this: Where?"

CHAPTER XXIX

Hanvey gazed at the gray walls of the jail and nodded as though having reached a startling conclusion.

"I believe our next move, John, is to have a talky-talk with Mister Maxwell Vernon."

"Good Lord! Has it taken you all this time to think of that?"

"Uh-huh. My brain was never strong on speed."

Reagan was earnest. "Quit kiddin', Jim. Why did you leave this palooka for the last?"

"Because I wanted to hear what everybody else had to say. From what you tell me, Vernon is lying high, wide and handsome, and I wanted to form some idea about what was truth and what wasn't."

"Sensible enough. Let's go."

Back into the brilliance of the warden's office, and thence down the dimly lighted corridor on which were the rooms used for those prisoners who seemed entitled to something better than the ordinary cells. The turnkey admitted them to a room identical with the ones occupied by Tony Peyton and Larry Welch. They stood in the doorway and Hanvey regarded the occupant through sleepy, half-closed eyes.

Vernon was seated on his cot. He had doffed coat and tie, and his shirt was open at the throat. His long black

hair was somewhat tousled and his chubby face wore an
expression of belligerence. His whole manner—even before a word was spoken—was combative, and he merely
murmured a curt word of acknowledgment when Reagan
introduced Jim Hanvey.

Jim seated himself in the rocker and smiled lazily at
the prisoner. He felt rather sorry for the boy, fat, good-
natured, easy-going . . . and now suddenly enmeshed in a
tragedy which he couldn't quite understand. He knew the
type; friendly, whole-hearted, too weak to say No—and
then abruptly trapped by his very good-fellowship. Jim's
voice came soothingly.

"Things been happening pretty fast, ain't they, Son?"

Vernon looked up sharply. "What things?"

"Oh, plenty."

"I don't know what you mean."

"Shuh! Sure you do."

Max rose and tried to look dignified. He succeeded
only in appearing somewhat ludicrous and entirely pitiful.

"I haven't anything to say, Mr. Hanvey."

"Well, what do you know about that? I haven't asked
you anything, have I?"

"No, but—"

"Listen to me, Son: answer me one question."

"What is it?"

"Did you kill Pat Thayer?"

Vernon's eyes closed. He pulled himself together with
a visible effort.

"No."

"Then I think you better talk to me plain and honest.
Of course, if you *did* kill him, the best thing you can do is
keep your mouth shut. Now—what say you?"

"Nothing. I don't trust any detective."

"And you ain't so awful far wrong on that, either. But
I'm a bum detective, see?"

"I don't care what kind of a detective you are. I'm not going to talk."

"A' right. I ain't gonna argue with you." He reached inevitably for the golden toothpick. "Swell new car you got, Son."

Vernon was stonily silent.

"Swell car," repeated Hanvey. "Sure wish I could own one like that. But I wouldn't go buy one just after I'd had a row with another man."

"I didn't row with anybody."

"No? Not even Pat Thayer?"

Max was trembling. Boyishly, he was struggling to keep actual tears from his eyes. "You're trying to trap me! I know! And I'm not going to say anything. Not anything at all!"

"That's up to you, Son. But suppose you tell me this: What happened between you and Thayer in the fraternity house day before yesterday about one o'clock in the afternoon?"

"In the fraternity house? Nothing happened."

"You went to his room, didn't you?"

"No."

"Aw, Son! You know dog-gone good and well you went to Pat Thayer's room. Now why don't you tell us what happened?"

"I didn't go near his room," cried Vernon harshly. "I went to my own room and changed my clothes, and then I left the house. I never saw Thayer all the time I was in there."

Jim shook his big head. "I hate to see you fighting me, Son, when I'm trying to help—"

"Like hell you are! You're trying to mix me up in Pat Thayer's murder."

"I'm trying to get the truth. Does that mix you up?"

"No, but—"

"Just before you went to the fraternity house, you and Thayer had a big row on the campus, didn't you?"

"Who says so?"

"Several people. And also there ain't much question that you were pretty sore at him. Now I ask you this: Why?"

"I had reason enough. I thought he was my friend. I've been buddies with him for two years. He's been winning all my money at cards. I guess I would have been a dumbbell all my life if I hadn't got sore at him over something else."

"Stealing your girl, for instance?"

Max looked up sharply, and became boyishly dignified. "I—I'd really rather not talk about that angle of it, Mr. Hanvey," he said gently.

"As you say, Vernon. But when this other thing happened—you getting sore—what then?"

"I started thinking—for the first time. And I began to suspect that it wasn't all just accident that Thayer had been nice to me so long as I had money; but the minute I went broke he lost interest in me and started going with . . . that is, doing things to make me sore. And it struck me that it was queer he had always won at cards. Then I remembered all the nasty rumors I had heard about why he had been invited to leave two other colleges—"

"You think he had been cheating you?"

"I know it. Oh! I was stupid enough, but I waked up all at once."

"And you got about as mad as you ever were in your life."

The boy's face was white. "Yes."

"You went to Thayer's room in the fraternity house—"

"I did not! I told you before I never went near his room."

"So you did. I thought maybe you'd remembered that you were mistaken. Anyway, you were in the house at the

same time he was. After awhile you left there hurriedly
with a bundle under your arm, didn't you?"

"I don't remember."

"What was in that bundle, Vernon?"

Max was nervous; his pudgy hands were twisted together and his eyes roved helplessly around the little room.

"A—a suit of clothes. The one I said I changed. I was
taking it to the Marland Tailoring Company for alteration
and cleaning."

"Good. Now we're clearing up parts of the mystery."
Jim turned to Reagan. "Suppose you check up on that,
John. Just 'phone that company and make sure they have
the suit, will you?"

"Sure." Reagan started to rise, but Max Vernon stopped
him. The boy's eyes were round with fear and beads of
perspiration stood out on his forehead.

"Never mind," he said hoarsely. "The clothes are not
there."

"You didn't take them?"

"N-n-no."

"Where are they?"

"I—I don't know. I guess I—I—lost them."

"You sure are an unfortunate young man," murmured
Jim. "Losing a good suit of clothes that way. Well, anyway,
after losing that suit, you drove on up to Steel City, didn't
you?"

Again Vernon hesitated. Then he nodded.

"Yes."

"Alone?"

Max's cheeks were pasty. "Yes. Alone."

"And when you got there you traded in your car on a
new one, didn't you? And paid the difference of twelve
hundred dollars in cash. Is that right?"

"Yes."

"Where did you get the money?"

"I have plenty of money."

"But you just said a minute ago that Thayer laid off you because you were broke. How could you be broke and also have plenty of money?"

"I had it. . . . I got it from Thayer. He owed it to me."

"I see." Jim beamed approval. "That clears up another mystery. You and Thayer were really friends, after all. He loaned you the twelve hundred dollars just like it was nothing, eh?"

"He gave it to me. He owed it."

"When did he give it to you, Vernon? When you went to his room?"

"I told you I didn't go to his room."

"I see. I guess he sent it to you by special messenger or something. Never mind that, though: It ain't any more important than the suit of clothes you lost. But there is one thing I want to know: How did it happen that there wasn't any floor rug in the car you traded when you got to Steel City?"

Again that hunted, haunted light in Max's eyes.

"I don't know anything about any floor rug."

"Wasn't there one in your old car?"

"I don't know."

"Gee! You sure are a forgetful guy. Now what about that knife Mr. Reagan showed you an hour or so ago? That is yours, isn't it?"

"Yes."

"Where did you get it?"

"In Sicily. I've traveled a lot and I've always collected queer weapons."

"Did you have it in your hand at all day before yesterday?"

"No."

"Do you know it is the very knife with which Thayer was killed?"

"I know that's what Mr. Reagan said. But I didn't have it."

"You knew it wasn't on your wall where you always kept it, didn't you?"

"No! How was I to notice that one of the things was gone? And I didn't kill Pat Thayer, Mr. Hanvey. I swear I didn't."

Hanvey spoke softly. "Admitting that, Vernon: Why did you get mixed up in the robbery of the Marland National Bank?"

Max stood rigid for a moment, then sank down on the cot. He buried his face in his hands. "I didn't have anything to do with that, either, Mr. Hanvey: honest I didn't."

CHAPTER XXX

The two detectives faced each other solemnly in the warden's office: Hanvey red-faced, complaining and not at all
excited; Reagan alert, admiring and critical.

"Will you tell me why," he asked—"when you had Vernon on the run, you didn't chase him?"

Jim shrugged. "Why? There wasn't any use scaring the
poor kid to death."

"You knew he was lying, didn't you?"

"Sure, John—sure. And the more questions I asked the
more lies he was gonna tell."

"Well, I'll say this for you, Jim Hanvey: You seem
to rock along with all the delicacy of an elephant—but
damned if you haven't learned a heap about this case."

"What, for instance?" inquired Hanvey interestsedly.

"In the first place, it's a cinch that Max Vernon did it."

"Did what?"

"Killed Pat Thayer."

"You think so?"

"Sure. Don't you?"

"Durned if I know, John. I couldn't say for sure, anyway. There's still a lot of loose ends."

"There always are on a case like this," snapped Reagan.
"Whenever a big crime happens we run out and grab all
the facts we can. They all look important because we don't

know which from what, but after we look into it we see
that some of the things we thought were important really
don't mean anything—and so we forget 'em. That's the
way in this case: we've got Max Vernon dead to rights. Any
jury would convict him."

Jim nodded heavily. "They certainly would. That's what
makes it so tough on the kid—provided he's innocent."

Reagan changed his tactics. He pointed an accusing
finger at Hanvey. "Anyway, Jim—you think he was mixed
up in that bank robbery, don't you?"

The fat man reflected for a moment, then nodded.
"Yeh—I do."

"And that," exulted Reagan, "is the first definite admission I've gotten out of you yet."

Jim smiled. "I am dumb, ain't I, John? Suppose you tell
me just how you think this murder happened. Just sketch
things over, will you, so they'll take their proper places in
my mind."

"Good enough." Reagan whipped out his notebook and
consulted it. "May first; eleven-thirty: Tony Peyton runs
across her husband making love to the kid sister of the man
she's crazy about. Big row. Thayer sore and Tony desperate.
Fifteen minutes later, after she's gone, Ivy Welch and Pat
Thayer meet Max Vernon. Thayer has been trimming Vernon for two years and the kid has just got good and wise
because Thayer went too far when he copped Max's girl.
Another quarrel. While that is happening, Tony Peyton is
warning Larry Welch that his sister is in trouble, and telling him why. He's goofy about her and it don't make him
feel good to know that she's married to this bird Thayer.

"At half-past twelve Pat Thayer gets to the fraternity
house and goes to his room. Five minutes later Max Vernon comes in. He's sore as a goat and when the two kids
on the veranda tell him Thayer's in his room, he says he
don't give a damn. And maybe he didn't then, Jim—but

don't forget that he had found out where Thayer was, and he had just quarreled with the man over a girl.

"Vernon goes to his room. He has been broke and worried. Some way—Lord knows how—he's entered into a deal with somebody to rob the Marland National Bank. He's nervous and desperate. He decides to go and have it out with Thayer right there. Thayer is a bigger man and stronger, and so Vernon grabs that stiletto off the wall to have it handy in case trouble comes.

"Meanwhile Tony Peyton has come in to warn Pat he must lay off Ivy Welch. I believe every word of her story of the visit. She beats it, and right after she does, Vernon goes into Thayer's room. He's got himself hopped up to a million and he talks cold turkey to Thayer. Thayer probably starts the fight. Vernon takes a wild swipe at him and the knife cuts his jugular vein. Vernon's cock-eyed scared. He beats it back to his room and pitches the knife in the corner of his clothes closet. Then he changes his clothes because the suit he had on when he killed Thayer was all covered with blood—which is why he never went to that tailor at all.

"Then he beats it to take part in that bank robbery. He gets to the bank corner just about two o'clock. The stick-up guy gives him the high sign and goes in, knowing that Max is waiting in his high-powered, speedy car to make a get-away. During the robbery the man is shot. While Max is driving him he bleeds all over the back of the car, so on the way to Steel City they stop and Vernon gets rid of his bloody suit and the floor rug. Then he takes his share of the hundred thousand berries that they've copped from the bank.

"He trades in his old car and is fool enough to think he's got a good alibi. Anyway, he's got too much sense to stay away from the University because he knows he'll be grabbed. Maybe he's worrying about what became of the knife. But a couple of minutes after he sets foot in his room at the fraternity house, the man on duty grabs him and calls me." Reagan closed his notebook and returned it to his pocket. "Ain't that a good case, Jim?"

The big man nodded slow approval.

"Durn near perfect," he applauded.

"What's wrong with it?"

"Nothing. . . . Nothing wrong with that story, John—not a single thing. Only how come Thayer was alive when Larry Welch got there at two o'clock?"

"Hell!" snapped Reagan. "He wasn't. Thayer was dead then. But Larry knew Tony had been there and he didn't know anything about Max Vernon. So he thinks Tony Peyton killed Thayer and shields her. Cinch, ain't it?"

"It seems so. . . . And the ring Ivy had given Pat Thayer?"

"Larry Welch took it. Didn't want his sister mixed up in the mess. Don't you see how clear everything is?"

"Uh-huh." Hanvey sighed profusely. "It's so dog-gone clear I'm scared of it."

"I'm not. I'm sorry for Max Vernon, of course. There ain't anything bad about the kid. Just weak. And he'd had a stack of money he thought would last forever. I've seen guys like him before: when they get desperate they're pretty bad medicine, Jim."

"I guess so. . . ." He was silent for a moment, then looked up brightly. "What'd you do with all the stuff Vernon had in his pockets when he was arrested?"

"Right here. Want to see it?"

"Yeh. . . ."

Five minutes later Reagan returned to the room. He spread out on the table the contents of Vernon's pockets: a handkerchief, a fountain pen, a notebook, several visiting cards, a fraternity pin, a bunch of keys, a Monte Carlo ten-franc chip which Vernon had always carried as a lucky piece, less than two dollars in silver, a packet of cigarettes and a box of matches.

Hanvey fumbled with the collection. "This all, John?"

"Everything except his wrist watch."

"Didn't he have a wallet?"

"Yeh." Reagan flushed. "It's in a special box in the warden's safe. Nothing in it but some money."

"How much?"

"Two hundred and ten dollars. I'll get it—"

"Never mind." Jim was holding the bunch of keys in his hand. Finally he imprisoned one of the keys between his thumb and first finger. "Doesn't this look like a new key, John?"

Reagan nodded.

"Sure does."

"Bank box, I'll bet," observed Hanvey, as though talking to himself. "Uh-huh, new bank box key." He looked around. "Anxious to do me a favor?"

"Anything you want."

"When's the next train for Steel City?"

Reagan consulted his watch. "Midnight."

"I hate to ask you, John . . . but I wonder if you'd run up there to-morrow alone?"

"Sure I will. The train carries a sleeper. They drop it in the yards at Steel City. I can be back to-morrow evening. What's the big idea?"

Jim detached the key from the ring. "Take this with you, John. I've got a hunch that Max Vernon rented a box at some big Steel City bank on the first, or maybe yesterday morning. Take some samples of his handwriting with you, because he'd use an assumed name of course. You can check up on all boxes rented in the last couple of days—then compare the handwriting."

"And if I find the box?"

"Just let me know."

"Shall I take a look inside?"

"No-o. There's a heap of red tape attached to getting in somebody's bank box. We'll just take it for granted that if he rented a box there the Marland Bank money is in it—or, anyway, Vernon's share. What say?"

Reagan rose. "I'm on my way, Chief." At the door he turned. "And if we do find that cash, Jim—and it turns out to be Vernon who had it—will you admit then that I was right?"

Jim smiled broadly. "Maybe," he said. "I'll sure think you were pretty near right, anyway."

CHAPTER XXXI

Warm brilliant sunshine bathed the courtyard when Tony Peyton and Larry Welch walked out on bond to temporary freedom. The small, wiry, kindly President was there; and the grizzled Dean, and three of Larry's faculty associates. There was Ivy Welch, seeming a great deal older than she had four days previously, yet irrepressibly youthful withal; and a score of Larry's undergraduate friends. There were sorority sisters of Tony's and another dozen young men and women who had come down to congratulate the young couple on what every one considered the end of their jeopardy.

Ivy was particularly happy. "They wouldn't have let you out if they thought you were guilty, would they, Larry?"

He shook his head. "I don't believe so, Sis."

"Good!" She clasped her hands. "All the time you were in there, Bud, I couldn't think of anything except—except—"

He squeezed her hand. "Don't you worry, Kid. I didn't have anything to do with it."

Tony was with a group of her particular friends and Larry nodded toward her.

"Why don't you and she make up, Sis?"

Ivy's face grew stern. "I don't like her, Larry."

"Why?"

"Because she started all this. If she hadn't butted in on Pat and me; if she hadn't run to you; if she hadn't been such a fool as to go to Pat's room at the fraternity house. . . . Oh! can't you see, Larry, that I can't help believing Pat never would have been killed if she had minded her own business?"

"I'm sorry you feel that way, Sis. You know I'm crazy about her."

Ivy sighed. "I guess I'm just a crab, Bud. But if I feel that way—well, I can't help it, can I?" Then she reached out impulsively and pressed his lingers. "Maybe I'll get over it."

Several automobiles were waiting, and at the request of the President, Larry rode to the college with that dignitary and Dean Boyd. They discussed the case gravely and told Larry a great many things about Max Vernon which he had not known. They themselves did not know many details, but the campus was overflowing with rumor. Larry was doubtful.

"It doesn't seem possible that Max would do a thing like that."

"And it didn't seem possible that you or Miss Peyton would, either. We have been mighty worried."

"You've been darn white to me. I intend to resign—so the college won't suffer."

The two older men smiled.

"We're sorry for the scandal, of course, Larry. But we can't accept your resignation—for two reasons: One is that we believe you are innocent. The second is that it wouldn't help you particularly—if you ever came to trial—if we had acknowledged our lack of confidence by permitting you to leave the faculty."

And later that day Larry and Tony met by Old Main and walked toward Pine Top . . . a knoll which rose above

the surrounding country and from which one could look
down upon the Marland campus, and thence still farther
to the sprawling town of Marland. Half the student body
saw them together and every young man and woman made
a point of waving cordially, but no one joined them. The
students were more than a little embarrassed. They wanted
the pair to know that there was every belief in their innocence, every sympathy, every willingness to do whatever
was necessary by way of help . . . but there was a natural
hesitancy in intruding on their privacy. The tragedy had
cast a sort of ghastly mantle about them.

They reached Pine Top and stood regarding each other:
the man tall and blond and very boyish-looking despite
the tiny lines of worry about his eyes; the girl vividly
beautiful. Their hands were clasped and they drank deep
of the wine of freedom and of their joy at being with each
other again. It was Tony who spoke.

"You know how I feel, Larry, about what you did."

He frowned. "What did I do?"

"Telling those detectives that Pat was alive when you
left his room. Of course I know he wasn't."

Larry's cheeks blanched.

"How do you know?"

A slow, sweet smile played briefly about the corners of
her lips.

"I know now, Larry. That's all I wanted: To trick an
admission from you. It was fine of you, dear. But we must
go to Mr. Hanvey and tell him the truth."

"The truth?"

"That Pat was already dead when you reached his room."

"But I didn't say—"

"Oh, yes you did, Larry. Just a second ago. Now listen to me: I don't know what you think about him—but
I believe that terrible-looking Mr. Hanvey is one of the

most wonderful men I have ever met. He can tell when
we're telling the truth, and he knows when we're lying.
Don't ask me how I know that—I just do. I told him the
truth, dear—even when it looked like I was tightening a
noose around your neck. I was scared—and yet I wasn't
scared. Everything I said seemed to increase your danger.
Mr. Hanvey looked like he had gone to sleep, and Mr.
Reagan . . . he isn't so bad, but I'm glad he's not alone on
the case. Then the next thing we knew we were released on
bond. Mr. Hanvey knows a lot. And if he's going to help
us, we must help him."

He nodded slowly. "I guess you're right." His face was
very serious. "It's kind of tough on Max Vernon, isn't it?"

"I'm sorry for that boy. Terribly sorry. And yet if killing is ever justified, it was then. We have no right, Larry,
to keep the truth from a man like Mr. Hanvey, who is
struggling to help us."

"We'll tell him."

They stood in silence for several minutes. Overhead
a mocking bird trilled gayly; the pine trees swayed and
sighed softly in the warm breeze which swept in from the
countryside. The air was freighted with the fragrance of
flowers and on Pine Top there was no suggestion of anything but ineffable peace and happiness. It was so different from the solitary confinement at the Marland jail; so
gloriously a relief from the staring at four blank walls and
a tiny square of barred window. They were very young and
very much in love with each other, and Larry moved so
close to her that their bodies touched.

"When all this is over, Tony, you will marry me?"

She looked straight into his eyes.

"Yes, Larry."

"I'd like to put into words . . . to be able to tell you
how much I love you. . . ."

"You don't need to. I understand."

His arms closed about her and he held her close, staring hungrily into her eyes. Then, suddenly, he buried his face in her hair and so they stood for an age of time. . . .

All that afternoon the campus hummed with crazy rumor and wild conjecture. It was one thing to read in the newspapers of a murder and quite another to come in contact with one. The students were impressed by their own importance in having known intimately the dead man and the three suspects. Then there was a feeling of depression, as though the college had been sullied. And the Psi Tau Theta boys went around with chips on their shoulders . . . although nobody dared utter a word of criticism.

The tragedy had cast a pall over the campus; yet it had brought a new and strange excitement. Even Commencement, which at this season of the year usually loomed up as being all-important, seemed a matter of little moment. Examinations held terrors for very few of the students. It was as though they had been confronted by some of the starkness of life a month ahead of time. Human life, human love . . . examinations and Bachelors' degrees seemed of small moment by comparison.

The afternoon dragged away. Larry worked over his class books, trying to rid himself of the effects of the experience and wondering what the future had in store for Tony, for himself, and for Max Vernon. And in his room at the hotel, Jim Hanvey sprawled on the bed and devoured a detective story.

It was there that John Reagan found him. Jim put the book aside reluctantly.

"Gosh," he commented, "it's great—that story. I'd sure like to meet a dick like that feller. Lemme tell you how it happened, John, and see if you can guess—"

"Hell—no." Reagan was practical. "I got plenty to tell you."

"All right." Jim sighed and closed his book. "Just as soon as I get interested in something like this, you have to come butting in. What is it?"

Reagan spoke crisply. "On the morning of May second a man answering Max Vernon's description—and there ain't any doubt, Jim, that it was Vernon—entered the American National Bank of Steel City and rented a box. He gave the name of William T. Aragon. I had a half dozen samples of Vernon's handwriting with me and there couldn't be any mistake. He took the box with him into a little booth. He also had a satchel—just the same sort of satchel Randolph Fiske says the bank robber had. Then he left the bank. The box is number two-thirty-five, and unless I'm all wrong you'll find a lot of Brother Fiske's lost money right there."

"Good work, John. You didn't look in the box."

"No. You said not to. But I left word that no one was to be allowed in there, even with a written order from Aragon. That's fixed good and tight. And so—"

The telephone buzzed and Hanvey answered.

"This is the warden at the jail," announced the voice at the other end. "Miss Peyton and Mr. Welch are down here. They want to see you as soon as possible."

"Send 'em over to the hotel, will you?" Then he turned away from the telephone and grinned boyishly at his friend.

"Welch and Miss Peyton are on their way over, John. Stick around if you want. I have a hunch we're going to hear some interesting dope."

CHAPTER XXXII

Tony Peyton acted as spokesman.

"Larry and I have been talking pretty seriously, Mr. Hanvey. We've decided that you're playing square and are entitled to have the whole truth—so far as we know it."

Jim's big face beamed. "That's fine, Miss Peyton. But I want to ask one thing before we start: Am I going to get the whole truth or only part of it?"

"The whole thing."

"Great! Suppose you begin."

She shook her head. "I haven't a thing to add to what I told you at the jail. That was the plain, unvarnished truth. I can't take anything from it—or add to it. I hope you believe me."

"Gosh! Miss Peyton—I couldn't help believing you, could I?"

"I think you know the truth by instinct," she said gently. "That's why I told it to you in the first place."

"It's a pity your boy friend didn't get the same hunch. We'd maybe have let him out earlier."

"I was a fool, I suppose," broke in Larry. "But I had reasons. . . ."

"What were they?"

"Well, in the first place, I knew I was innocent and thought you'd never be able to convict me. So I wasn't very

much of a hero after all. In the second place, I was a trifle
frightened."

"By what?"

"By the thing you've known all the time: that Pat Thayer
was dead when I went to his room at two o'clock on May
first."

"And, of course, you thought Miss Peyton had done it?"

"No-o. . . . I was apprehensive, of course. I couldn't
imagine her doing a thing like that, but then—well, she
says she has told you all the circumstances—between herself and Thayer. . . ."

"Sure. She told us."

"Knowing that she had been there and that she was
desperate—and seeing Thayer dead—I had every reason to
be afraid."

"Sure you did. But after you found out that Max Vernon had also visited Thayer's room, why didn't you tell us
the truth?"

"I was still nervous. Suppose I had said Thayer was
dead when I was there and you had believed me? And then
suppose it turned out that Vernon had never visited the
room? Can't you see that it would have checked it back to
Miss Peyton beyond any argument?"

"Yeh. . . . That's right, sure enough. I'm mighty much
obliged, Son, for clearing all these things up in my mind.
And now suppose you tell me about that visit?"

"There isn't much to tell. I had promised Miss Peyton that I wouldn't go to see Thayer until after she had a
chance to talk with him. But I did see my sister Ivy. I was
rather appalled by the depth of her infatuation for Thayer.
I was in a peculiar position, in that I had promised Miss
Peyton I wouldn't tell any one about her marriage to
Thayer. I figured that by that time—two o'clock—she had
had plenty of chance to see Pat and I felt it was up to me,
as Ivy's brother, to warn him off."

"You were sore?"

"Good and plenty. Naturally, I would be."

"What did you have in mind when you went to Thayer's room?"

The young man hesitated. "I'm trying to be honest, Mr. Hanvey, and the fairest way to answer that question is to say I don't know. I haven't been in a fight since I was a kid. Even in football games where the going has been pretty tough, I've kept my head. But it's only honest to say that I intended to make it mighty clear to Thayer that he'd better keep away from Ivy."

"I see. . . . And when you got there?"

"He was dead. I got rather sick, just looking at the body."

"Did you touch him?"

"Good God! No!"

"What did you do?"

"I turned around and walked downstairs again."

"How long were you in the room?"

"I don't know. Maybe two minutes, maybe ten. I can't remember. It must have been several minutes, though, because it seemed as though for a while I couldn't think at all."

"Did you shut the door when you left the room?"

"I don't remember. I felt pretty scared."

"Why didn't you report finding the body?"

"Because I thought of Miss Peyton."

Hanvey nodded approval. "Pretty straight story, Welch. There are just one or two more questions. First of all, did you touch the knife?"

Larry's face expressed surprise.

"What knife?"

"The knife Thayer had been killed with."

"I didn't see any knife."

"Did it strike you as queer that Thayer was dead and there wasn't any knife there?"

"I didn't think about that. It never occurred to me to look for a weapon."

"I see. . . ." Jim extracted a black cigar from his vest pocket, snapped the end from it and lighted the thing with a brief nod of apology to Tony. "You took that diamond ring off Thayer's finger, didn't you?"

Again that startled light flashed in Larry's blue eyes.

"I told you I didn't touch the body at all."

"Aw, come now, Son. You promised to tell me the whole truth, and it don't hardly seem like you're doing it. Why not slip me the straight dope on that? Nothing could have been more natural. You find the body of the man your sister is crazy about. He's been killed. On his finger is a diamond ring that can be traced back to your sister easy. It means mixing her up in a pretty nasty affair. So you take the ring off Thayer's finger and keep quiet about it. Ain't that the way it was?"

"No," said Larry firmly, "it wasn't. I never noticed Thayer's fingers at all. I can't say what I would have done if I'd seen the ring. But I didn't see it, and that's the truth."

"Well—" Hanvey heaved a vast sigh. "Somebody did—because it's gone."

"I didn't touch it," repeated Larry. "I hope you believe me."

"I reckon I do. And I'm much obliged for coming here. Though I can't say it has cleared things up a whole lot."

They chatted for a few minutes longer and Larry and the girl left. Reagan closed the door behind them and faced his ponderous companion.

"You believe Thayer was dead when Welch got to the room, Hanvey?"

Jim's big head bobbed slow affirmation.

"Looks pretty straight to me."

"You don't think Miss Peyton killed him, do you?"

"Gee! I'd sure hate to think anything like that about such a swell kid as her."

"Did Welch take his sister's ring off Thayer's finger?"

"Now you've got me stumped. I'm durned if I know."

"What do you think?"

"My thinks ain't worth nothing, John. What do you think?"

"He did not. The man who copped that ring was Max Vernon. And why? Because he was crazy about Ivy Welch and knew her ring. Gosh! Jim—even a guy like you must be ready to admit now that Max Vernon killed Thayer."

"Why should I admit that, John?" asked Hanvey mildly.

"Because he killed him, that's why. There ain't any argument about it."

"Why ain't there?"

"Oh, hell! We've got Vernon a hundred different ways. It's as clear—"

"—As mud."

"Well, suppose you tell me just one thing that ain't clear?" Reagan was quite positive in his manner. Hanvey smiled broadly through a cloud of rancid smoke.

"The first thing I can't straighten out in my mind, John, is the knife that we found in Vernon's room; the one that we're sure Thayer was stabbed with."

"What about it?" Reagan's cheeks were red. "I overlooked it on my first search, that's all."

"Think so, John? You ain't such a bum searcher as all that, are you?"

"Any man can miss something. I overlooked that knife, that's all. And knowing it was his, and finding it in his closet, is enough to convict him."

"No," argued Hanvey gently. "It's enough to acquit him, John."

"What the—"

"Now listen, Brother, and don't get all het up. According to your own pet theory, Max Vernon carried that knife into Thayer's room and stabbed him during a row. Then he carried it back to his room and had sense enough to polish the fingerprints off the handle—because, remember, there wasn't a print on it. He then changed his blood-stained clothes. And then, by golly, you ask me to believe that a bird who was careful as all that went out and forgot the knife! Holy suffering mackerel! John—that just ain't reasonable. It don't click. Yeh, it's the knife that worries me, and it would worry you too, if you'd get off that one-track railroad you're riding. The knife is Max Vernon's only chance. If it wasn't for that I'd bet he killed Thayer."

Reagan was pop-eyed as the idea slowly percolated.

"Then—then you think that knife was planted in Max Vernon's room?"

Jim regarded the end of his cigar speculatively. "I sort of have a hunch that way, John. Think it over." He hoisted himself from his chair and waddled to the door. "Let's ride over to the college, if you don't mind. I want to see a lot of folks."

"Who?"

"Well, I ain't talked with those two kids who saw everything from the porch—Farnum and Gleason, ain't they? And I'd like to talk with the Dean again, and maybe the president of that fraternity. And most of all I'd like to have a few words with Ivy Welch."

CHAPTER XXXIII

That night Jim brought misery to the soul of John Reagan by forcing him into a motion picture theater. The screen story—rather well done—was saccharine, and Reagan was amazed to see Hanvey dab at his eyes occasionally with a cheap, cotton handkerchief. The fat man did not relax during the entire picture: he exulted with the hero and did everything but hiss the villain. When it was over he emitted a large sigh.

"Gosh, John! Wasn't it wonderful!"

"Hooey!" snapped the hard-boiled Reagan.

Jim turned sorrowful eyes upon him. "Ain't you got any sentiment, John? Not any at all?"

"Maybe you have, Jim. I just don't make you out at all. You're good—I can see that. But darned if you don't take the most roundabout methods . . . anyway, now, about this case—"

"No, John—not to-night. I don't like to talk about murder when I've just seen a beautiful picture like that one in yonder." He imprisoned Reagan's arm. "Let's go."

"Where?"

"For a chocolate ice cream soda."

"Good God!" exclaimed Reagan. But he went.

The following morning Hanvey was dressed when Reagan arrived, and at the former's suggestion they went to

the jail and were admitted to Max Vernon's cell. The boy
looked more haggard than when they had last seen him.
His pudgy cheeks seemed to sag, his eyes had a wild, hunted look and his manner was piteously belligerent. Hanvey
addressed him in a voice more stern than Reagan had yet
heard.

"I'm talking straight from the shoulder, Vernon," said
Jim firmly, though not unkindly. "You're in the hottest
kind of hot water. It'd be so easy to convict you of Pat
Thayer's murder that a kid could do it."

"I didn't kill him."

"Maybe not. But, oh gosh! all the evidence says you did,
and it's evidence that a man gets convicted on. Now I'm
trying to help you. Believe it or not—I am. I'm out to get
the man who killed Thayer—and if it's you, then I'm after
you. If it isn't, I'm anxious to turn you loose. I'm going to
get some definite action to-day. Heap quick, see? I'm giving you this last chance. I can be your friend if you'll let
me. And the way to let me is to tell the whole truth from
beginning to end—nothing held back. If you don't do that
we'll put you over the jumps for the murder of Pat Thayer.
Think it over, Kid, and tell me how it looks."

The boy rose and walked up and down his tiny cell.
Tragedy was stamped grotesquely on his boyish face. It was
obvious that he was battling with himself for the thou-
sandth time. Once he made a remark, without facing his
accuser.

"I didn't kill Thayer."

"No? Well, maybe not. But you were mixed up in the
robbery of the Marland National Bank!"

Max whirled. "Who says—"

"Steady, Son! It's the truth I'm after, and the truth I'm
going to have. I've got you checked up on the Marland
Bank thing. Maybe it'll satisfy you if I mention the name
of William T. Aragon."

The boy's face blanched, and out of the silence came Jim's voice again—infinitely gentle.

"Robbery ain't half as rotten a charge as murder, Max."

Vernon stopped his pacing. His shoulders were sagging as he turned back to Hanvey.

"You win," he said dully.

"You'll tell the truth?"

"Yes."

"All of it? Every bit?"

"Yes."

"All right, Son. Shoot!"

"I—I'll try to make it brief, Mr. Hanvey." Vernon was almost eager. It was as though a load had weighed him down so heavily that there was a relief in getting rid of it, no matter what the consequences. "I've been a damned fool—but not a murderer."

He paused and Jim prompted quietly—"Yes . . . ?"

"Pat Thayer and I have been friends since he first came to Marland as a junior last year. I was a sophomore then. I looked up to him, and thought he was wonderful. I didn't suspect then that his interest was not in me, but in my money. I was always a fool—if that's what you'd call a free spender, and it seemed like I'd always do what Thayer wanted me to.

"Over a period of almost two scholastic years he has been trimming me. We played two-handed stud. Of course I never suspected that he wasn't on the level. Meanwhile, this year, it happened that I went crazy about a girl. It doesn't matter what her name is—"

"You mean Ivy Welch?"

"Yes, Ivy. I'm awful fond of her. And this spring Thayer took me for my last cent. I guess I had thought my money wouldn't ever give out . . . and the first thing I knew I was broke. I had lost about forty thousand dollars in two years to Pat Thayer. Even then I wouldn't have suspected

him if his whole attitude hadn't changed. He had my note
for five thousand dollars. I didn't have a dime to pay him,
and I couldn't borrow. The president of the Marland bank,
who I thought was a friend of mine, refused to lend me
anything. Then, when Thayer knew I was stripped, he did
everything in the world to show that he had contempt for
me. He dazzled Ivy Welch—not because he liked her, but
because he seemed to take a delight in doing everything to
make me miserable.

"Dumb as I was, I began to wake up. I looked back over
all our card games and commenced to see things I never
would have suspected if Thayer had remained halfway decent. I may be wrong, Mr. Hanvey, but I'd almost swear
that Thayer had been cheating."

"I don't think you are wrong, Max."

"On May first I had a date with Ivy. I was to meet her
by the south gate of the Bowl. She stood me up. I wasn't
very happy anyway, and that made me feel worse. Then
when I saw her coming up the hill with Pat Thayer I sort
of went crazy. I guess it's the first time in my life I was
ever completely mad.

"We had a quarrel—Thayer and I. When I left him I
was in a cold sweat. If you want to know just how I felt, I
guess I was mad enough to kill him. Maybe I'd have done
it if I'd thought about it—but I didn't. All the way across
the campus I was trembling so I could hardly walk. I guess
I was madder at myself for being a fool than I was with
Pat for what he had done. I got in my car and went off.
It's a wonder I didn't kill myself the way I drove. I thought
it would cool me down, but it didn't. And I made up my
mind I'd go to town that night and get lit; just plain cock-
eyed drunk. You see, I'm telling you all the truth. Every
bit of it, Mr. Hanvey."

"Go ahead, Son. You're doing swell."

"I got to the fraternity house and Rube Farnum and Phil Gleason were sitting on the porch. They're nice fellers but kind of crazy. They made some friendly remark about Pat Thayer being up in his room and I guess I cut them off pretty short because when I went in the house I heard them whistle and make some comment about it being the first time they'd ever seen me mad.

"I went straight up to my room. That's on the third floor. Thayer's room is on the second. I changed my clothes and I shaved. Then I decided to take the suit I had had on to the tailor. I wanted it cleaned and some new pockets put in. I don't know how long I was in the room, because I was still sort of dizzy, I was so sore. I didn't leave my room until I walked downstairs. I had the suit rolled up in a bundle and had it under my arm. Then I got in the car in front of the Psi Tau Theta house and drove off toward Marland. I stopped on the way to get gas. Then I was going down Archer Street to Oak, where the tailor is. I got to the corner about half-past two o'clock, as near as I can remember.

"There is a traffic light on that corner, Mr. Hanvey, and it flashed red just as I got there. I stopped for it because there's always a cop there who grabs Archer Street motorists who run over the red light. And it seemed almost as soon as I stopped that something started in that bank."

The boy was speaking swiftly now—and graphically. He was looking straight at Hanvey, and his black eyes were blazing.

"Shooting started inside that bank. I don't know how much shooting, but it sounded like a lot, and I was scared to death. Then all of a sudden the door opened and a little man ran out. He was carrying a satchel. I had been too scared to move—just sitting in my car with the motor running.

"This man—he was the robber—jumped in the back of my car and flopped on the floor. I was pretty near paralyzed, I was so scared. And I got a heap more frightened just about two seconds later."

"Yes? What happened, Max?"

"That feller in the back of my car stuck a revolver right against my neck. He was all crouched down, I think. Anyway, there wasn't any mistake about the revolver.

"'I've just robbed that bank,' he said, 'and I'm damn desperate. Now drive—and drive fast.'"

"And you?" asked Jim.

"I drove," answered Max Vernon simply. "And I drove fast."

He stopped talking.

"Hadn't you ever seen this man before?"

"No. Not until he ran out of the bank and jumped into my car."

"And all you have told me is the strict truth?"

"Yes." The boy hesitated. Then he looked levelly into Hanvey's kindly eyes. "But it isn't all the truth, Mr. Hanvey. I'll go on with the story if you don't mind."

"Please do, Son," murmured Jim. "And try to remember that me and John Reagan are your friends."

CHAPTER XXXIV

"I guess it seems funny," continued the young man, "that I'd help a robber escape, but I could feel that gun stuck against the back of my neck. . . . And once, just before we got to Birmingham he told me to skirt it. He said he was hiding in the back so he wouldn't be seen and I was to act natural. He said if I signaled anybody or tried to pull any fancy stuff, he'd kill me, because he'd just as leave be grabbed for murder as for robbery, and he said he had most likely killed a man in the bank anyway. He told me to drive around the city and stop at a place by the Little Indian River." He faced Reagan. "You know where I mean, don't you, Mr. Reagan? It used to be a sort of picnic ground."

The detective nodded. "Yeh, I know. Road dips off to the right and goes down to some bluffs that overlook the river."

"That's the place. It's about twenty minutes' drive beyond the city limits. Anyway, I did just like I was told. All the way through the suburbs the man in the back of my car didn't say a word, but I didn't think anything of that because he had said he wouldn't. I was awfully afraid the police had telephoned everywhere about the Marland bank being robbed and I would be stopped, but nobody said a word.

"I got out into the open country again and speeded up, and still not another word from the back of the car, but I was just as scared as though the gun was stuck into my neck. When I got to the turn-off place by the Little Indian, it happened that there weren't any other cars in sight and I know no one saw me turn off. I went down that road—I guess it hadn't been used in a long time because it was awful rutty. And when you get on it there are a lot of trees and bushes so that a car is invisible from the road after it's gone about a hundred feet. Down near the river bank the car couldn't be seen from anywhere except the other side of the river, and I guess it's wider there than anywhere else.

"I stopped the car and cut off the motor. I was afraid to look around. But when about a minute passed and he didn't say anything, I spoke to him. 'Is this the place you wanted?' I asked. He didn't answer, and I spoke to him again—I don't remember exactly what I said. And he didn't answer this time, either.

"I didn't know what to make of it, and I was scared to turn around for fear he'd shoot me. I had been pretty frightened of that anyway, because I knew all about him and I thought he might figure it was better to kill me, too, to get my evidence out of the way. After a while, when he still didn't speak, I looked around, sort of expecting that he had run away."

Vernon was talking swiftly and his face was twitching with excitement.

"He was there, Mr. Hanvey. He was lying all huddled up in the bottom of the car and the first thing I saw was a lot of blood. I knew he was unconscious and that I was safe. I started to run away, but then I got scared. I was so scared that I suppose I acted more bravely than I would have done otherwise. I went back to the car and opened the tonneau door. I took his gun, which was lying on the floor of the car where he had dropped it, and for the first time I felt safe.

"I looked at him a long time, feeling pretty sick. It was the first time I had ever seen anything like that. It was maybe ten minutes before I dared touch the body . . . anyway, I finally did. And I saw that he was dead!"

The boy ceased speaking abruptly. His cheeks were white, and occasionally he closed his eyes as though to shut out the grisly picture. Hanvey sat relaxed in his chair, a half smile on his lips, as though applauding Vernon for his straightforward story.

"There wasn't any question that he was dead. I got more courage. I felt for his pulse and it had stopped. I put my hand on his heart. It was still. I even got up enough nerve to put my ear close to his mouth to see if I could get the faintest sound of breathing—but there wasn't any. Then a new idea hit me all of a sudden. I wondered what would happen if somebody found me parked in the woods with the dead body of a man. There was the gun, too, and some bullets had been fired from it and it might look as though I had killed him.

"I opened the little satchel. And then I got almost as much of a shock as I did when I first saw the body. It was crammed and jammed with money. Paper money. It was more money than I had ever seen before." The boy hesitated and his hands clasped and unclasped nervously. "I don't know why I ever thought of such a thing, Mr. Hanvey; but right then I did."

"What, Son?"

"Of keeping that money. I guess it's hard to make you gentlemen understand, but all my life I have had money. I am an orphan and when I came to college I had almost a hundred thousand dollars. It had always seemed as though that money would last forever. I spent it foolishly, and then Pat Thayer had virtually stolen a huge amount from me. I was broke and worried. I owed Thayer five thousand dollars, and I didn't know then that he was dead. I hadn't ever worked and didn't know how. Being broke scared me.

"I—I don't think I'm bad, Mr. Hanvey. I've never in my life done a crooked thing, and I thought I never would. I wouldn't have helped to rob a bank. I wouldn't have stolen a nickel. But it seemed as though this money was just miraculously given to me.

"The robber was dead. No matter what they knew about him, they couldn't possibly think I had anything to do with the robbery. I suppose you think I'm a fool . . . but it did seem different— then—keeping the money that was there, and stealing it from the bank. I suppose I was trying to argue myself into it. I should have returned to the bank and told them . . . anyway, I'm telling the truth, and the truth is that I didn't." He paused, then went on bravely. "I kept the money. I intended to keep it always. It looked as though with what I had learned about foolish spending, I'd be protected for life, and I thought no one would ever suspect.

"The man in the back of the car was dead. He had been killed robbing a bank. I was afraid of being found with him, anyway. I—I weighted his body with some towing rope I had in the car and two big stones and threw it in the river. The floor rug was stained with blood. I threw that in, too. The clothes I had intended to take to the tailor were also covered with blood, and they were thrown in the river. Then I hid the satchel under the back seat and drove on to Steel City.

"I hardly knew what I felt like then, Mr. Hanvey. I was scared and nervous—and yet I was elated. It seemed like my troubles had ended. I didn't like to remember what I had done with the body . . . but I consoled myself with the fact that he was merely a robber. I knew I had done wrong, but it didn't seem as though it was very wrong. I told myself that I had taken the money from a dead body . . . that is, I tried to think that it wasn't the bank's money anyway. They had already lost it. And I even remembered that banks are insured against that sort of thing."

"They are," said Hanvey. "I sort of represent the insurers."

"I guess you know the rest. I got to Steel City and looked at a new car. I wouldn't have done that ordinarily, but I felt as though I'd be nervous driving my old one, on account of what had happened in it. Then the next morning I bought the car and paid the difference in cash. I kept a few hundred dollars in my pocket and then hired a safe deposit box in the name of William T. Aragon. I figured the money would be safe there. Then I come back to Marland—and they arrested me almost as soon as I reached the fraternity house."

His voice trailed off. He looked at Reagan's granite countenance and then at Hanvey's fat, kindly one.

"That's the truth," he said with a note of desperate appeal in his voice. "I swear to God it is."

Jim's bulbous head inclined slowly. "You had a pretty tough time, didn't you, Son?"

The note of paternal sympathy in the voice of the detective affected the boy strangely. A mist covered his eyes and he dabbed at it with a handkerchief. Hanvey continued, as though he hadn't noticed the emotion of the young man:

"How much did you take out of the stolen money, Max?"

"About sixteen hundred dollars, including what I paid on the car."

"And all the rest is in the Aragon box?"

"Yes, sir. Every cent."

"How much is it altogether?"

"I don't know, sir. I was scared to count it even in the hotel. I thought somebody might be looking through a keyhole, or something like that."

"Sure. . . ." Jim detached his golden toothpick from the hawser which held it. He eyed it speculatively and seemed to speak to it rather than to Max Vernon.

"Son," he said, "I sort of think you've talked mighty straight with me. I'm not a regular dick, you know. I'm down here on this bank business and it sure makes me feel good to get that sort of straightened out. As for you—I think you've learned a heap of lessons. 'Bout all you'll ever need 'til Kingdom Come. Ain't that so?"

"Yes, sir. Yes. . . ." Max choked.

"In some cases my organization will chase a guy all over the world for the sake of putting him in jail. We'd have done the actual robber that way. Other times we're durn human, provided we don't lose any cash by it. Now I'll make a deal with you: Suppose we say that I'm to return to the Marland bank all the money that's left. They'll take your note for the missing sixteen hundred—and you're to get a job and work hard to pay it back. Maybe they'll take your new car and call it square. You're to leave college and try to make something decent of yourself. And in return for that, Max Vernon, I'll turn you loose. What say?"

"Mr. Hanvey! You mean . . ." The lad's face was radiant with happiness. He was almost incoherent in his gratitude. And John Reagan's voice broke in coldly.

"Just a minute, Hanvey. That's all very well about the robbery stuff . . . but what about the murder of Pat Thayer?"

Jim Hanvey chuckled softly.

"Shuh! John—I could have told you long ago that Max Vernon didn't kill Thayer. Only reason I didn't turn him loose on that charge was because my job down here was first of all to get at the bottom of the bank robbery. Now that I've done that I don't see any use holding an innocent man." He turned smilingly to Vernon. "As soon as I actually get the cash, Son, and fix things up with the Marland bank, we'll send you out to make a good, useful citizen of yourself."

Vernon's chubby face was glowing. But Reagan sat in the corner shaking his head.

"What I'd like to know," he growled, "is who the devil killed Thayer?"

CHAPTER XXXV

It was an unusual spectacle—that meeting in the office of the President of Marland University; a thing strangely grim and unacademic. The President sat gravely at his desk. He had begged to be excused, fearing the intrusion, but Hanvey had insisted that he remain because the matter directly affected the reputation of the University. And so the President sat there, looking decidedly ill at ease, and gazing with some wonder on the assemblage.

At the door stood John Reagan, the muscular and decidedly efficient policeman. He *would* stand by the door, reflected the President with a flash of inward humor; just as though some one might try to escape.

Next to Reagan was the lanky but not ungraceful figure of Teddy Farrell, President of the Student Council, President of Psi Tau Theta and a track man of no mean ability. He tried to appear languidly at ease, and made a sad botch of the job. He didn't know why they wanted him anyway. The affair was bad enough for the fraternity without insisting upon his presence in an official capacity.

Beside him, incongruously enough, was Mike Carmicino, janitor at the fraternity house. Mike looked and felt distinctly out of place, but he said nothing. He was considerably awed by the presence of the college President.

By his side was Rube Farnum, solemn as an owl, but
with an irrepressible roguish light in his eyes; and beside
Rube was the dynamic Phil Gleason—somewhat subdued
for the moment. Next to Phil was the trim little figure of
Ivy Welch in ridiculously short skirts, rolled stockings and
a general air of depression. Ivy, considerably older than
she had been a week previously, looked unusually serious.
She stared at the floor and had nothing to say to any one. It
was as though she considered herself a very important cog
in the machinery which was shortly to be put in motion.

Larry Welch occupied the seat next to his sister. His
unruly blond hair gave him an appealingly youthful look,
which the stern set of his features belied. He was solici-
tous of Ivy's welfare and occasionally his eyes met the pair
on the other side—those of Tony Peyton.

Tony showed the strain under which she had labored;
and she gave evidence, too, of the annoyance which had
been caused by the unpleasant publicity. Of course the
students and faculty had been more than kind to her; but
their very solicitude had rasped her nerves until she felt
that all she wanted now was to get off somewhere alone.

Through the open windows came the drone of campus
sounds: students laughing and chatting, all unmindful of
the drama being enacted on the second floor of Old Main;
an occasional shout; once in a while the scratch of an
automobile starter and then the hum of its motor. The
breeze which sighed in through the window was freighted
with the fragrance of summer. It fanned the cheeks of the
youngsters and seemed only to bring greater discomfort to
the mountainous man who completely dominated the scene.

Jim Hanvey was standing beside the President's desk,
puffing—without shame or apology—upon one of his noxious cheroots. He, himself, did not appear particularly
happy, and his first words were couched in an apologetic
tone.

"Folks," he said gently, "I'm doing something here that I swore I'd never do. I've got you all lined up like a theayter to hear what I've got to say about this case. I feel awful silly—but I guess it's better to tell everybody at once and have you all get it straight than to run around whispering to one at a time." He mopped his neck quite violently, and started again.

"I'll make things about as brief as I can, and I'll start with the most important. I guess all of you have heard about how we had Max Vernon dead to rights. Well, folks, that was all a lot of hooey. Max didn't have no more to do with killing Pat Thayer than I did, and—"

He was interrupted by a shout of glee from Rube Farnum as that lanky individual leaped across the floor and pumped Vernon's hand. He was closely followed by Gleason and Teddy Farrell, but Jim waved the others back and continued his recital. His sleepy, half-closed eyes missed no detail: the startled expression on the faces of Tony Peyton and Larry Welch—the inquiring looks flashed toward them by the others as he bluntly exonerated Max Vernon.

"About Max," he went on smoothly—"him and me have got a little secret which nobody is gonna find out about. Ain't that a fact, Son?"

"Yes, sir." Vernon's voice was almost a whisper and he was dangerously close to tears. The others looked away sympathetically.

"And now for Miss Peyton. I reckon rumors can't be kept down very well around a school like this, and so I suppose you've all heard that she was Pat Thayer's wife—that is, that they went through a sort of ceremony last year. She didn't want to say anything about that, but I explained it would be best because you-all were talking anyway, and you'd never have understood why she went to Thayer's room on May Day. What she went for, folks, was to settle a little personal matter with Thayer—and to let him know that his hold over her was broken: that is, that from then on the campus would have to know that she was legally his wife.

"What happened up there is nobody's business. Not even mine. But I'll tell you this much"—and he grinned infectiously—"Tony Peyton didn't kill Pat Thayer—and that's a fact."

There was a gasp. Larry Welch was sitting forward tensely, his eyes focused on Jim's placid face. The others stared at him in doubt and fear. Was it possible . . . ? Only three suspects and two of them already had been cleared by the words of the detective in charge of the case.

Impulsively Ivy reached for her brother's hand. It was cold as ice. And as though from a great distance, she heard Hanvey's words.

"And now we'll discuss Larry Welch's part in this, little affair."

He paused—whether from a consciousness of the dramatic, or because the heat had rendered him somewhat limp—it was difficult to say.

"I guess I ain't giving any secrets away when I announce that Larry and Miss Peyton have been kind of goofy about each other for a long time. Also I think it's pretty common knowledge around the school that Pat Thayer had been rushing Miss Welch, Larry's sister."

A red stain dyed Ivy's cheeks and she bit her lip.

"On May first," went on Hanvey, "Larry Welch learned two important things. The first was that Pat Thayer was the husband of the girl he was crazy about. The second was that the man his sister was going with was a married man. And as soon as he found out those two things, he went to see that man.

"I've got a reason for telling you all that, folks. The truth might be embarrassing sometimes, but it never hurts, and if I held anything back, you might either think we didn't have all the facts or else you might put two and two together and make a million. Larry and Miss Peyton have given me permission to tell all this, and they don't care whether the students hear it or not—provided they hear the straight truth, see?"

There was a tense, breathless nodding of heads. Jim smiled reassuringly toward Larry.

"Just what might have happened between Welch and Thayer nobody will ever know," he said smoothly. "Because when Larry Welch got to that room, folks—Pat Thayer was already dead!"

There was a nerve-racking hush; then a buzz of conjecture. It wasn't Max Vernon; it wasn't Tony Peyton; it wasn't Larry Welch . . . but Pat Thayer was dead. He had been stabbed in the throat on the first day of May and his body had been found on the floor.

"You see," grinned Jim, "I'm a queer sort of a bird. Seems like all I can accomplish on a case is to find out who didn't do something. I reckon you-all think I haven't had a bit of luck finding out who did. Ain't that a fact?"

They were too astonished to do more than stare.

"It's a cinch Thayer didn't kill himself. And if neither Vernon nor Miss Peyton killed him and he was dead when Larry Welch got there—then somebody killed him between times. Now we have Mr. Farnum and Mr. Gleason here to prove that nobody else entered that fraternity house through the front door during that time. Of course they could have come in the back way—and gone out by the same route.

"But that is hard stuff to find out, and I guess it's up to me to get a little dope on who did this thing. Else I guess you'd think I am as rotten a detective as I think myself. How about it, Larry?"

Larry gave him a weak nod. Hanvey surveyed the group in his quiet, friendly manner. His somnolent eyes lighted on the face of Mike Carmicino, the janitor, and even though he did not call the man's name, every person in the room knew to whom he was speaking.

"You and Mr. Thayer were pretty good friends, weren't you?"

Carmicino's eyes flashed to Jim's face.

"Yes, sir, Meester Hanvey."

"You told me that you did bootlegging jobs together: that he would get the orders and you would supply the liquor. That's true, isn't it?"

"Yes, sir." Mike's tongue moistened his lips. . . .

"The last time you worked together that way, Mike, was a few days before the killing. You told Mr. Reagan and myself that Mr. Thayer never paid you until after he had collected the money—and you further said that he had paid you for the liquor furnished on that last party. Is that true?"

"Yes, sir. He don't owe me no money, Meester Hanvey."

Jim turned to Teddy Farrell, president of the fraternity.

"You were in charge of the finances of that particular party, weren't you, Mr. Farrell?"

"Yes, sir."

"Have you ever paid either Pat Thayer or Mike Carmicino the two hundred dollars that the liquor was supposed to cost?"

"No, sir. I still have the money. It was never paid to either of them."

There was just the faintest hint of iron in Jim's voice as he turned back to the startled janitor.

"You lied about that, Carmicino!" he accused. "And I want to know why!"

CHAPTER XXXVI

Suddenly and fiercely, without the slightest warning, the entire aspect of the case had altered. All eyes were bent now upon the figure of Mike Carmicino, who sat tensely on the edge of his chair, eyes blazing defiance. His long black hair was tousled, his rather fine features distorted with fear.

Yet he did not become voluble. It was obvious to even the most inexperienced that he was weighing his words; desperately seeking to escape from a net which he felt was being tightened about him.

Jim Hanvey was patient enough. And finally Carmicino's eyes lighted and he gave a pleasant smile and a soft answer.

"I told you lie about Meester Thayer," he suggested suavely, "because he was good friend of mine."

"I see. . . . Just what do you mean, Mike?"

"Meester Thayer he always pay me as soon he gets the money when the fellers they have parties. This time he has not got the money when he is killed and so I think it is not nice that I should tell about how he owed me the money when he is dead."

Jim nodded heavy approval. Others breathed more easily and relaxed. Mike cast a golden smile of triumph about the room.

"I was only protect' my friend, you see, Meester Hanvey."

"Good for you, Mike. Mighty fine of you." Hanvey thought for a moment and then: "But isn't it true that Thayer had held out on you on other occasions and that you had several quarrels? Isn't it true that this time he announced he wasn't going to pay you at all and would turn you over to the police for bootlegging if you dared squawk?"

Carmicino's manner was one of outraged innocence.

"No, Meester Hanvey—that is not so. Meester Thayer was ver' fine feller."

"Isn't it true," persisted Jim, "that you and he were partners in the criminal occupation of obtaining and selling liquor and that when he threatened to turn you over to the police you very rightly considered that he was violating the code of the underworld . . . that he was double-crossing you?"

"That is entirely not true, Meester Hanvey."

The portly detective appeared baffled. Carmicino radiated good humor—a sort of taut good humor—but nevertheless he seemed at peace with the world.

"Maybe you're right about that, Mike. But how about the knife with which Thayer was killed?"

Carmicino's smile was dissipated for a moment, and when it reappeared, seemed rather forced.

"What about it?" he asked softly.

"Just this," said Hanvey in a calmly conversational tone. "Thayer double-crossed you. He didn't have the money then but he told you flatly that he intended to keep it, and you could go whistle—or else. You were sore as a goat and you said he couldn't get away with any such stuff." Hanvey was now making statements rather than asking questions. "You saw him go to his room on May first and you decided to have it out with him. But you knew you were dealing with a larger man than yourself and one who evidently wouldn't scare worth soup. So you remembered the collection of weapons in Max Vernon's room and borrowed the likeliest one—which happened to be that Sicilian dagger.

"You saw Miss Peyton go to Thayer's room and waited until she had left the house. Then you went in. You had a quarrel and finally a fight. You killed Thayer because he threatened to squeal and also, perhaps, because he attacked you. You left his room immediately. But you had sense enough not to make your discovery of the body until some one else entered the room. You didn't squawk when Max Vernon went into Thayer's room for the simple reason that Vernon never went there. But Larry Welch did go—and found the body. As soon as he left you let out a howl. It was real slick of you, Mike, because no one ever thought that the man who found the body was the murderer."

Carmicino was sitting in rigid silence. There was a fierce play of expression on the swarthy face, and it was plain that he was holding himself in check with a violent effort.

At the door John Reagan was tense, his beady eyes never leaving Carmicino's face. He was watching like a hawk—ready to intercept any move toward escape. The others were too startled by the sudden change of events to do more than stare first at Mike Carmicino and then at the impassive, immobile face of his accuser.

"Later on," continued Hanvey smoothly, "when the whole fraternity house was buzzing with comment about the murder, you heard the name of Max Vernon frequently mentioned. You also knew that he had disappeared. It was not until you heard that he was under suspicion that you thought of the knife. Mr. Reagan, yonder, had already searched that room thoroughly. And after his search you planted the knife in Vernon's clothes closet, knowing that it would be a mighty strong piece of evidence against him. So you see, I've got you kind of hog-tied, Mike."

Carmicino's face was stony.

"You can't prove none of that, Meester Hanvey."

Jim smiled triumphantly.

"Oh! yes, I can."

"How?"

"Because," announced Hanvey quietly, "your finger-prints are on the handle of the knife."

Carmicino leaped to his feet. "That is a lie!"; he shout-ed. "There were not any fingerprints on that knife!"

And now the Gargantuan detective became positively friendly. His words dripped honey.

"How did you know that, Mike?"

The spectators did not quite understand the byplay; but they knew from Carmicino's flash of terror that some-thing vital had occurred.

"You see," explained Hanvey smoothly, "nobody but Reagan and myself knew anything about whether the knife had fingerprints on it. Just ourselves—and the murderer. But *he* knew! *You* knew, Mike, because you very, very care-fully polished all the fingerprints off that handle! I think we've got you, Mister Carmicino."

"You—you can't convict me on that kind of evidence," said Mike weakly.

"I think we can. Mighty easily. But even that, Mike, isn't all I've got against you. I have one more piece of evi-dence. Just one, but it will prove a great deal."

He plunged a big fist into his bulging coat pocket and took therefrom a diamond ring. He waddled across the room and came to a halt before Ivy Welch, and toward her he extended the gleaming, flashing bit of jewelry.

"Ever seen that ring before, Miss Welch?"

The girl's voice was trembling, but she answered with-out hesitation.

"Yes, sir."

"Where did you see it last?"

"I put it on Mr. Thayer's finger myself several days before he—before he died. It is my ring."

"Mr. Thayer never returned it to you?"

"No, sir. He promised never to take it off his finger."

"Good!" Jim smiled genially. "You see, folks, that little ring is mighty important. It was not on Thayer's finger when the police got there. It was, in fact, stolen by whoever killed Pat Thayer. And that ring, folks, was found by me personally where Mister Mike Carmicino had very carefully hidden it!"

Carmicino was quivering. His eyes, distended with horror, were staring at the impassive face of the detective. And then, something like a howl of animal terror escaped from his lips. He leaped to his feet and broke forth into a torrent of words. His eyes rolled, his body twitched—

"Yes, I kill Thayer. I kill him, Meester Hanvey—but I swear it was only after he attack' me. He attack' me and hit me and then I swing with the knife and I do not intend to kill him but he fall down and there is much blood. . . ."

"That's all right, Mike." Hanvey's voice was gentle. "I'm glad you admit it was you. And if you can prove that it really was self-defense, maybe you'll have a chance." He turned to the others and bowed with elephantine grace. "I reckon that's all . . . and I'm much obliged to every one."

They crowded about him and shook his hand. He blushed like a schoolgirl and fairly shooed them from the room. Reagan slipped a pair of handcuffs over Carmicino's wrists and then telephoned Marland headquarters. Within twenty minutes two plainclothes men arrived in a touring car and the janitor was entrusted to their care.

Alone with Hanvey, John Reagan turned to stare.

"I'll be everlastingly damned," he said slowly. "There wasn't hardly a minute, Jim, that I didn't think you were just plain blundering dumb."

"Shuh! John—I ain't so smart."

"Like thunder you ain't. Man, I'm grateful. Only for you I'd have sent Max Vernon up for that thing, and even if I am a cop, I ain't keen about convicting an innocent person."

"I figured that, John. . . . Well, I'm hot and tired. Let's beat it."

Reagan continued to display his astonishment. Then his eye fell upon a scintillating something which Jim was holding between thumb and forefinger.

"Gosh, Jim," said Reagan, "you forgot to give Ivy Welch her ring."

"No-o . . . I didn't forget."

"It ain't any of my business, Hanvey—but what are you keeping it for?"

"Because," explained Jim; "this ain't her ring."

"What?"

"Naw. I had to run a bluff, Reagan. You see, the kid is a good scout. She wanted the guilty man caught and was willing to help me. She went to the city with me and helped me select an imitation which looked pretty much like the one she had given Thayer—and which had disappeared. Of course, the bluff happened to work, and it yanked a confession out of Carmicino. I always was lucky, John."

"Lucky? You're a wonder!"

The blade of Jim Hanvey's golden toothpick clicked shut. The mammoth detective sighed deeply and started for the door.

"We've got just one more job, John," he said, "and then I'll hop the rattler for cooler weather."

"What's the job, Jim?"

And Hanvey grinned like a schoolboy.

"We'll have to search through Mike Carmicino's things until we really find Ivy's ring," he said. "Let's go!"

THE STUDIO
MURDER MYSTERY
THE EDINGTONS

MURDER
AT SEA

RICHARD CONNELL

THE SEVEN BLACK
CHESSMEN
John Huntingdon

SMOKE
SCREEN

Lawrence Saunders

COACHWHIP PUBLICATIONS

COACHWHIPBOOKS.COM

NOVEMBER JOE

DETECTIVE OF THE WOODS

H. HESKETH-PRICHARD

MURDER
IN A WALLED TOWN
KATHERINE WOODS

THE LAST TRUMPET
A HUGH RENNERT MYSTERY

TODD DOWNING

JOHNNY ON THE SPOT
AMEN DELL

COACHWHIP PUBLICATIONS

COACHWHIPBOOKS.COM

FEAR OF FEAR

FLORENCE RYERSON
COLIN CLEMENTS

MURDER IN THE FAMILY

NICE PEOPLE MURDER

Mary Hastings Bradley

3 DETECTIVES
FEMMES AUDACIEUSES
MERWIN • SOMERVILLE • FOOTNER

DEATH DOWN EAST

Eleanor Blake

COACHWHIP PUBLICATIONS

COACHWHIPBOOKS.COM

THE
MYSTERY
OF THE
FOLDED
PAPER

HULBERT
FOOTNER

The
Hollow Tree
Mystery

MADELON ST. DENIS

VIRGINIA RATH

DEATH AT
DAYTON'S FOLLY

No Face to
Murder

EDITH HOWIE

COACHWHIP PUBLICATIONS

COACHWHIPBOOKS.COM

THE QUINNY HITE
MYSTERIES
CHINESE RED · HERE LIES THE BODY

RICHARD BURKE

The Black Gardenia
Elliot Paul

WHITE
FOR A
SHROUD

DONALD CLOUGH CAMERON

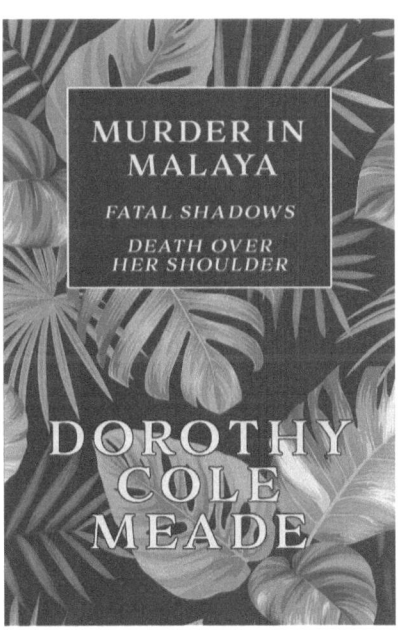

MURDER IN
MALAYA
FATAL SHADOWS
*DEATH OVER
HER SHOULDER*

DOROTHY
COLE
MEADE

COACHWHIP PUBLICATIONS

COACHWHIPBOOKS.COM

COACHWHIP PUBLICATIONS

COACHWHIPBOOKS.COM

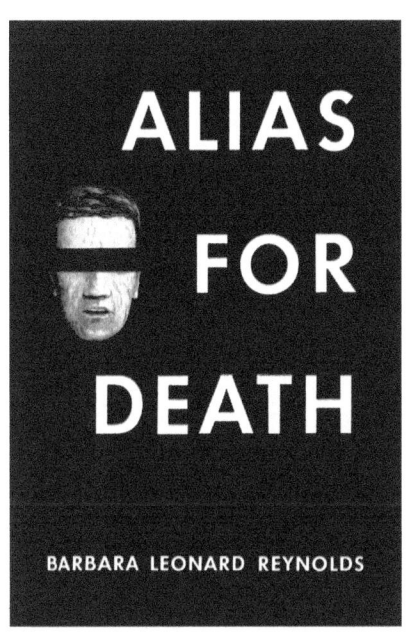

ALIAS FOR DEATH

BARBARA LEONARD REYNOLDS

THERE IS NO RETURN

THE ADELAIDE ADAMS MYSTERIES

ANITA BLACKMON

Jack Dolph

MURDER MAKES THE MARE GO

LADY IN LILAC

SUSANNAH SHANE

COACHWHIP PUBLICATIONS

COACHWHIPBOOKS.COM

www.ingramcontent.com/pod-product-compliance
Lightning Source LLC
Chambersburg PA
CBHW050508260626
47157CB00004B/1232